Beatrice Washington

The Story of Juliette

A Child's Romance

Beatrice Washington

The Story of Juliette
A Child's Romance

ISBN/EAN: 9783744766531

Printed in Europe, USA, Canada, Australia, Japan

Cover: Foto ©Andreas Hilbeck / pixelio.de

More available books at **www.hansebooks.com**

THE

STORY OF JULIETTE

A Child's Romance

BY

BEATRICE WASHINGTON

"Only a girl, — only seven." – JEAN INGELOW

ILLUSTRATED

BOSTON
ROBERTS BROTHERS
1892

CONTENTS.

———•———

LIST OF ILLUSTRATIONS.

STORY OF JULIETTE.

A CHILD'S ROMANCE.

— ◆ —

CHAPTER I.

HOW THE TRAVELLER CAME TO THE ENCHANTED CASTLE.

WHEN the sun sets in the emerald sea that dances along the shores of France, it turns the quaint little town of St. Servans into an Enchanted City; for the slanting rays of the sunset fall full upon it, and bathe the whole in a flood of gold. As the gleams catch

each slated roof or gilded weather-cock,
they splinter themselves into a thousand dazzling fragments, and each window sparkles like a diamond, or glows
like a ruby, while down in the harbor
the tall masts shoot up into the sky
like burnished spears, and below them,
in the dancing water, their reflections
writhe and twist, green and gold and
scarlet, like sea-serpents on fire.

Once a traveller got lost in the Enchanted City at sunset, and could not
find his way out of it. If he looked
toward the harbor, the sea and the sky
seemed a lake of light, and the myriad
masts rose out of it like flames, so that
his eyes were dazzled; and if he turned
his back on the sun, and looked up the
hill, the windows and the street-lamps
and the roofs, all flashed back the sunset
with such marvellous brilliancy that the

town seemed on fire. So he felt baffled on every side ; and though he was a shy traveller, and spoke French very badly, he made up his mind to ask the way.

For a long time he found no one to whom he could venture to address himself; for it was a fête day, and most of the people had gone over the hill to a fair in the next village, or were amusing themselves with the sailors in the harbor. So the traveller went on till he came to a crooked side-street that straggled up one side of the hill. The houses were irregularly built, and half-way up the slope they ceased altogether, and the road degenerated into a mere cart-track, and this again dwindled to a grassy foot-path that ran along by the side of an old wall. The traveller was just beginning to think himself less than ever likely to find a

guide in this deserted lane, when a
sudden turn of the path brought him
in front of a tall, iron gate, half buried
in a tangle of lanky nettles and morn-
ing-glories.   The bars were red with
rust; the curves and flourishes
of the scroll-work were
hung with cobwebs;
and the stone
vases which
crowned the
pillar on either
side had become
perfect wildernesses
of grass and poppies
and yellow moss.

Had the stranger been an artist, he
would have forgotten all about his
destination, and there and then filled
his sketch-book with "studies;" had he
been a poet, he would have mused over

the silent pathos of the ruins before him, and have written a poem on " The Threshold of the Past," or something quite as melancholy. But he was only a lawyer, and art and parchment do not agree, so he merely gave a very cursory glance to the picturesque gateway, and did what most likely the poet and the artist would have forgotten to do, — he tried to get through it.

But the gate was locked. The rusty bars were stronger than they seemed; and pull and shake as he might, our traveller only got his hands badly stung by the nettles, for his pains.

He was stooping to bind a dock-leaf round his smarting fingers, when he heard himself addressed in an imperious tone from the other side of the gate.

" Que voulez-vous, Monsieur ? "

The voice certainly came from within, yet he could see no one. He looked again through the twists and scrolls of the iron-work, but there was nothing to be seen, except the green path continued through a grove of laurels.

"Dites-donc!" said the imperious voice close beside him; "que voulez-vous, Monsieur?"

"Monsieur" turned sharply, but only to graze his elbow against a jutting angle of the wall. Certainly the voice came from that direction; and acting upon a happy thought, he squeezed himself close up against the opposite corner of the gate, and looked through it sideways toward the angle. There, in strong relief against the gray crumbling stones of the old wall, framed in the tangled wreaths of a pumpkin-vine, the traveller beheld the quaintest, prettiest picture he had ever seen.

Perched airily among the green fans of the pumpkin foliage, sat a little maiden, so small, yet so exquisitely proportioned that the traveller — had he not torn up and forgotten all his childish stories long ago — might have mistaken her for a fairy. She was dressed in a very simple little frock of faded green, that reached almost to her toes, and wore, instead of a cap, a yellow scarf tied over her brown curls. From this improvised cap, the hair broke loose in rich masses and clusters of dusky curls that floated over and around the little face like a cloud, and through the breezy tendrils that clustered about her forehead shone two dark shadowy eyes. Those eyes attracted and held a stranger's glance at once; but the traveller noticed also the rich coloring of cheeks and lips, and the delicate oval of the face.

He almost started, as he turned his
eyes to her companion; for there, ram-
pant among the great, yellow gourds
and dusty, green leaves, with two terrible
wings outspread, and one claw raised,
he beheld a fierce beast, known to him
in nursery days as a dragon. This
creature looked fully as forbidding as
the monsters of fairy lore. It was as
large as a mastiff, and with the excep-
tion of two ferocious, red eyes, was a
beautiful blue, streaked with green
stains, and mellowed by the touch of
time into an harmonious turquoise hue.

The traveller stared hard at this
curious pair; but the maiden and the
Dragon sat on serenely, — she with her
arms round his neck, and her curly head
reposing against one outstretched wing.
She seemed not at all surprised at the
ridiculous attitude of the stranger, — he

was squeezed up against the wall, gingerly holding on to the gate, with his face pressed close against the rusty bars; but presently she repeated her question in the same imperious tone.

Not knowing, or at least for the moment not remembering, what he did want there, the traveller replied, in his best French, " I have lost my way."

The little maiden rose, and pushing aside the pumpkin-leaves with tiny brown hands, came toward him saying slowly:

" They always do lose their way; but you have found it at last."

" Have I ? " he asked eagerly; " then who are you ? "

She stood quite still for a moment, with one little hand on the gate, looking up through the bars, and then threw back her head with a gesture of queenly disdain.

"Do you not know? I am an Enchanted Princess, and this is my keeper,
— the Dragon."

"Oh," said the traveller.

"I will let you in," went on the Princess, drawing a big key from her sash,
and fixing it, with some difficulty, into
the lock ; "but you have come too soon.
The Apples of Life are not ripe yet."

"No," said the traveller, rather sadly ;
"they will never ripen for me."

The Princess had pulled the gate
open now, and he went in, half curious,
half amused, and stood waiting while
she re-locked it, and put the key back
into her sash.   Then she held out her
hand, and he took it in his, and so they
went along the laurel-walk.

"They always ripen," said the small,
clear voice at his side, "when the King
comes.   But he is away; and you must

wait. When the King comes," she cried, joyously, clasping the hand she held, and smiling up at him through the tangle of curls, "the Apples of Life all turn to gold, and any one may pick them. You have only to wait for three weeks now; so you need not go back."

They had come out upon the deserted garden of an old French château. The gravel-drive was green with weeds; the flowers had left the *parterres* to run wild over the daisy-sprinkled lawn; and the rose-bushes trailed their sweet festoons across the path in charming but reckless confusion.

Beyond the lawn stood the ruins of

an old house, half covered with creepers.
The fire-tinted streamers of the Virginia
creeper waved from the gables, and
looped themselves across the shuttered
windows; the roses had begun an ad-
venturous ascent, and stopped half-way,
heaped up in glowing masses round the
pillars of the porch, or thrown across
the steps. Swallows darted from the
eaves to circle round the broken sun-
dial on the lawn; and a few white
pigeons spread their silver fans upon
the roof.

Was this the Enchanted Castle?
The Princess stepped along demurely
till they reached the closed door, and
then she pointed to a seat in the
porch.

"Sit there," she said, dusting the
stone with her little green gown; "I
will go and tell the Queen."

So the traveller sat alone in the rose-
covered porch before the closed door,
and the Princess ran away round
the corner of the deserted house,
through the sweetbrier hedge, and out
of sight.

CHAPTER II.

VIRGINIE, AND THE QUEEN, AND THE ENCHANTED PRINCESS.

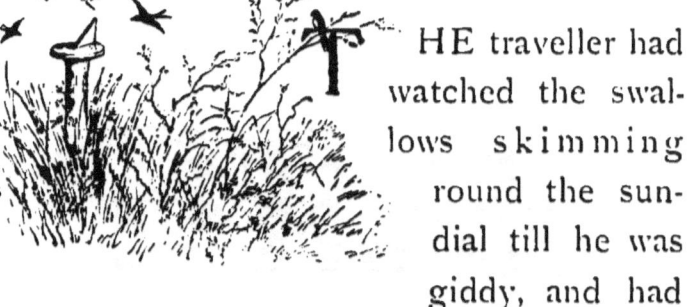

HE traveller had watched the swallows skimming round the sundial till he was giddy, and had counted the bees about the roses till he was tired, when the Princess came back. She held up her hands to keep the rays of the low sun from her eyes, and looked at the stranger from under its shadow.

"The Queen cannot come to you, for she is busy; but if you will come

with me I will show you the tree where
grow the Apples of Life," she said.

The traveller hesitated, fearing to
appear intrusive, and the little maiden
gazed at him thoughtfully.

"Of course, if you do not care, you
need not come; but I must let you out
or the Dragon will devour you. He
will know you are not the right sort.
Shall I let you out?"

"No, no; I should like to see the
Tree of Life."

"Then you must come this way;
take care you do not tear your coat."

The princess stepped deftly through
the hedge of sweetbrier; and the traveller, unused to such a thorny path,
scrambled through as best he could,
and received a good many pricks and
scratches in the process. They went
round the side of the house, and found

themselves on a little lawn, in the midst
of which stood a great apple-tree, with
gnarled roots and mossy boughs, weighed
down with ripening fruit. Round the
lawn grew smaller fruit trees and bushes,
and at the back spread a little kitchen-
garden. A clothes-line was slung from
one of the apple-boughs to a slender
cherry-tree, and under the line of fluttering linen stood a young girl in a
pink cotton dress, folding the snowy
garments and laying them in a basket.

"Virginie!" called the Princess, "here
is a traveller who has lost his way.
He is come to see the Tree of Life."

Virginie turned, and gave a little
start. She had expected to see some old
mendicant, not the young barrister who
stood at the edge of the lawn beside her
little sister, in evident embarrassment.

His confusion made her forget her

"VIRGINIE TURNED AND GAVE A LITTLE START."

own, and she advanced with a bright smile of welcome, and dropped the linen to hold out her hands in kindly French fashion.

" Bon soir, Monsieur ! " said Virginie.

Her face was just such another as that smiling up from under the Princess's shadowy curls, only more wide awake, more piquant. Here the dark eyes sparkled with animation, and the loose curls, gathered up into a classic knot, were streaked with gleams of gold. Perhaps the beauty was not so ideal, nor dreamy, but it was none the less charming.

" Pray — I — pray do not let me interrupt you," stammered the traveller, feeling that his French was atrocious, " I — we lost our way — I mean I lost mine — and — "

" No ; you have found it," said the

Princess, pointing to the apple-tree; "but you must wait till the King comes home. Then the apples will be gold."

Virginie laughed, and turned again to her clothes-line. When all the fresh, white linen was folded and laid away in the basket, and she had collected the little wooden pegs into her apron, she went over to the apple-tree, and stood leaning against a low branch, watching the stranger and the Princess. They were talking together quite amiably, and the Princess had bound up the torn hand in her little handkerchief.

"Come, Marie Juliette," said Virginie, "the sun has gone to sleep; it is time for bed."

"But here is the poor traveller;" replied the Princess, "where can he go? He is all alone in this country, he says."

"That reminds me," said the poor traveller, rising, "that I came here to ask my way, and lost it. Can you direct me to the Rue de la Courte Côte?"

Virginie considered with her pretty brows knit into a little perplexed frown.

"Yes — but I am afraid it is very — well — complicated; there are so many turns. Shall I show you the way?"

"A thousand thanks! But indeed I do not need to trouble you; I am sure I could find it."

"I don't think you could, for you don't speak French very well," said Virginie, with charming candor. "But I daresay I can come. If you will help me carry in that basket, we can ask my mother."

"Certainly," said the traveller, directly forgetting all about his torn hand;

and he looked down at the Princess, who was studying him thoughtfully.

"Shall I say good-night, then, Princess Juliette?"

"If you are going to see the Queen," said the Princess, "I think you had better wash your face."

The traveller grew very red, and Virginie laughed till the pegs rolled out of her apron; but the little maiden went on quite gravely, "It's where you squeezed yourself against the bars, to look through. The marks came off on your face."

"Never mind," said Virginie, picking up her clothes-pegs, "you can use the pump, if you like; and here's a clean cloth. See! — there is the pump, — under the scarlet-runner."

The young barrister, who had recovered his presence of mind, laughed good-humoredly, and agreed to the proposal; and the Princess worked the pump-handle with such vigor that his hair and clean collar were completely saturated: but one does not mind such trifles in an Enchanted Castle, especially if there are two charming maidens looking on, and a Queen in prospect.

When the operations under the pump were completed, the Princess led the way, across the lawn, to the back of the house; the others following with the basket. They came to an open door, beside which stood a wooden bench, a barrel of grain, and some gardening tools. Virginie went in with the basket, telling the others to wait for her. While they did so, the traveller noticed that this part of the house, at least, seemed inhabited. A white curtain fluttered from the open casement of a window

near him, and a tortoise-shell cat
crouched on the sill. Through the
door, which Virginie had left ajar, he
saw a high wooden dresser, and a table
covered with clean linen and ironing
implements, and the basket which
she had set down upon the red-tiled
floor.

Presently Virginie came back, followed by a pretty little Frenchwoman,
plump, dark-haired, and bright-eyed, with
a posy of mignonette pinned into the
big bib-apron that covered her gray
gown. She shook hands affably, and
smiled, her keen eyes taking in every
detail of the young barrister's face and
dress, as he stood up and bowed, with
his hat in his hand. Virginie had
made clear how matters stood, so he
was saved the difficulty of explaining
his position, and waited courteously for

Madame to speak, which she did somewhat volubly, but very prettily, offering
her daughters as guides, and pressing
him to take some refreshment, after
his search so fruitless, so mortifying, and
his loss of time so great. Refreshment
he refused; but the escort he received
with thanks, and evident pleasure.

" Hasten then, Virginie!" cried the
Queen, clapping her hands to empha-
size her words, "to conduct Monsieur
to his destination; and you, Marie
Juliette, pluck a grand bunch of roses
to offer to your friend. Quick, then!"

The sisters flew at her bidding, — Virginie indoors to fetch her hat and scarf,
and the Princess to the garden of roses,
to gather a posy from the porch.

" And it is on affairs of business you
are come to this country so strange to
you?" asked the Queen, filling her

apron with grain for the pigeons, as she spoke.

"Yes," he said; "it is to see about some property that has been left to me, — a little apple-farm in Normandy. I want to put it into repair, and take my mother there. She is the only one I have left; and she is dying."

Perhaps it was the kindly interest in Madame's eyes, perhaps it was the sympathy in Virginie's face, — she had come up, and was listening, — that had drawn him on to saying so much, for he was very reserved, as a rule, this traveller. But the spell of the Enchanted Castle was upon him, and it opened his heart, and loosened his tongue.

"Where did you say, Monsieur?" asked Virginie, softly. She had put on a big straw hat, tied under the chin

with a pink bow, and had thrown a soft
white scarf over her shoulders. She
looked like a Gainsborough picture,
only she did not know who
Gainsborough was, and the traveller himself knew very little
more.

" In Normandy," he said.

The Queen looked up and
sighed, and repeated wistfully
the words of the old song, —

" ' Oh ! ma Normandie ! ma Normandie ! '

I too, Monsieur, have my heart in Normandy. But it grows late ; there is
the moon high above the apple-tree.
I wish you all good fortune, my friend,
and health to the *bonne maman!* "

She held out her hands, wished him
good-night, and then went away to call
the pigeons.

Virginie looked up from the ground, where she had been tracing patterns with the point of her shoe, and said, "Let us come this way, Monsieur; there," with a little laugh, "you need crawl through the sweetbrier hedge."

But though she laughed there were tear-drops on her lashes, as she turned her face to the moonlight, and one fell on to the folds of her scarf and lay there gleaming softly.

"I am so sorry for you, Monsieur." she said frankly, shaking the tear away; "it is so sad to be all alone in the world! I am sad sometimes, though I am quite happy really, — I have a mother and a father and the Princess. But for you, with only one, and she to be dying — I am so sorry for you!"

"Thank you," said the traveller. simply. He was not given to many words.

By this time they were in the front
of the house, and the Princess, who had
climbed on to the sun-dial, got down,
and ran to meet them, with her hands
full of roses.

"See!" she called, holding up her
flowers, "these will do for a little time,
till the apples are ripe ; but you will
come back, when the King comes, —
won't you ?"

He took the posy and looked at it
absently. The flowers were lovely, —
great blooms of Gloire de Dijon and
Marichal Niel, exquisite damask buds,
and deep red roses with hearts of fire ;
here and there gleamed a white blos-
som, a globe of pale light lying like a
moonbeam among the glowing petals
round it.

"Why don't you speak?" cried the
Princess, impatiently, "you are not look-

ing at them at all, with your eyes. Perhaps you are thinking of the apples?"

The traveller laughed and held out the posy, to show off its beauties.

"I think they are lovely, Mademoiselle," he said.

Mademoiselle nodded graciously, and they all three went down the laurel-walk and out of the gate, which the Princess opened with her big key. There sat the blue Dragon, stately and grim in the moonlight, with the dew glittering on his terrible wings, and a moonbeam lying right across his nose. He made no attempt to devour the traveller, he did not even move his gaping jaws; but the Princess seemed to think it necessary all the same to hold up her tiny forefinger in warning and say, "Quiet there!" in an imperious tone.

This danger passed, they went along
the lane and down the hill and up again,
till, by various twists and turns, they
arrived at the Rue de la Courte Côte.
They did not talk much
on the way. There
seemed a silver si-
lence shed by the
moon over every-
thing. The golden
lake and the fiery
sky were pale and
still, and the masts

in the harbor looked like the shadows
of thin ghosts. The Enchanted City
was asleep, and down below the sea
murmured a quiet lullaby.

"Good-night," said Virginie, when
they had reached the hotel, and stood
on the steps waiting for the door to
open. "I wish you good luck, Mon-

sieur, and that your good mother may
recover, — and I hope you will be
happy."

" Good-by ! " cried the Princess, " don't
forget to put the roses in water ;
and remember about the Apples of
Life. You need not be afraid of the
Dragon, for I am nearly always at the
gate watching for the King, and for
stray travellers. You will not forget ? "

" No," he said, standing with bared
head to bid them good-by, " I will not
forget. And I thank you both very
much for your help, and for the
roses."

When they reached the end of the
street, and glanced back, he was
still standing on the step with the
roses in his hand. He looked after
them as they went down the hill,

in the moonlight, Virginie straight
and slim, and the Princess in her
quaint, green gown, and felt quite a
poet and an artist, — in spite of the
parchment.

CHAPTER III.

WHY THE BLUE DRAGON LEFT THE CHÂTEAU DE LAURIENNE.

WENTY years ago the Blue Dragon had sat in state, keeping guard over the treasures in the drawing-room of the Château de Laurienne. He had a right to his position; for he had been presented to the grandfather of M. le Comte by an English duke, for some service rendered by the Frenchman in his youth. Then

his blue coat had been spangled with
golden stars and moons, but now the
gilt had rubbed off even from his fierce
talons. Still he was very handsome, and
very aristocratic, and more than that
he was the gift of a duke.

The drawing-room was half in gloom,
for the green shutters were down in the
veranda, and the sunlight could only
filter in through chinks and crevices.
It flickered across the soft carpet, and
gilded the edges of the Louis Quinze
furniture, and lost itself among the folds
of silken curtains. Through the cool
darkness floated the scent of roses, and
the faint fragrance of pot-pourri.

But though the green shutters could
keep out the sunshine, they could not
keep out the sound of angry voices, nor
the tramp of footsteps hurriedly pacing
the terrace outside. M. le Comte and

his only son were quarrelling; the Blue
Dragon knew all about it for he had
seen them go out across the veranda
with hot, angry faces, and now he could
almost hear what they said. He even
knew more about it than they did themselves; for he knew how it would end,
and they did not. He had seen one or
two family quarrels in his lifetime, and
was wise in such matters. One does
not live a hundred and twenty years
without learning something, and by this
time the Blue Dragon was pretty well
acquainted with the De Laurienne
temperament.

It was the old story, for history re-
peats itself, though every one thinks
his own love tale a new one. Young
François de Laurienne had fallen in
love with the daughter of an apple-
farmer; her father's name was Petit,

and hers was Juliette. Now Petit may
be a very good name, but it has not a
De to it; and then there were the apple-
orchards ! Sometimes the aristocrat
has a long pedigree, and the bourgeois
has a long purse; then the De and the
money agree, and it is a good match.
But here there was neither De nor
money, only a respectable surname, and
half-a-dozen acres or so of apple-or-
chards; so that it was quite out of the
question that Juliette Petit should ever
become Juliette de Laurienne.

Thus argued M. le Comte. Not so
his son, — far from being out of the
question, it was the very way to set
matters right. Once she was Juliette
de Laurienne, there was no need whatever for the old name ; and if that were
objectionable, there was all the more
reason for changing it. As for the apple-

orchards, — they could stay where they were, and the farmer too. He did not want them, he only wanted Juliette.

As to whether the farmer had an opinion in the matter neither of the two cared; and François knew quite well what pretty Juliette thought. He had known so ever since the last apple-harvest, when they had looked at the moon through the orchard-boughs, and divided a Normandy pippin between them. He knew too, that she was sweet and true and gentle enough to be the mistress of half-a-dozen Châteaux de Laurienne.

But M. le Comte did not care in the least about harvest moons and true-love promises; he cared about family pride, and the family purse, and had an eye to the advantages of marrying his son to a distant cousin, the daughter of a

certain baron with a long pedigree and
a well-filled coffer.

So they were quarrelling furiously,
that summer afternoon, on the terrace,
and the Dragon sat in the
drawing-room and listened
to them.

It all ended
as he had fore-
seen. François
de Laurienne
the younger took mat-
ters into his own hands, and rode
away with pretty Juliette one early
autumn morning before the dew had
dried upon the orchard boughs. François de Laurienne the elder did not ride
after them ; he waited till Juliette Petit
was Juliette de Laurienne, and then he
quietly disinherited his son, and forbade
him ever to set foot within the Château.

4

So before the gloss had worn off the wedding gown, young Monsieur and Madame found themselves penniless, without a home, and without the means of making one. Happily for them, if somewhat unfortunately for himself, old Petit had indulged sometime since in a foolish speculation; for, on the persuasion of a fellow farmer, he had bought an old house which his friend owned at St. Servans. This house had proved as complete a failure to old Petit as it had to his friend; for, from some cause or other, no one had ever been induced to take it, and it seemed very likely that no one ever would.

Now, however, kind-hearted Monsieur Petit rejoiced in his dismal purchase, and offered the old place, rent-free, to the young couple. They could tidy it up, he said, and make the bit of garden pay; and as the house was larger than they needed, he suggested summer boarders as a nice, easy means of livelihood. Now all this sounds delightful, and François and Juliette thanked the good old farmer with tears in their eyes, and looked forward to an Arcadian existence, rendered remunerative by a kitchen-garden and summer boarders.

For the first two years all went happily. Old Petit came over from Normandy to do up the garden himself, and provided a superannuated couple, whom he had picked up on his way, as boarders. At the end of that time, the ancient couple dying and ceasing to require summer lodgings, the rooms became empty once more; and François, who was not cut out for a gardener, and had contrived to kill nearly all his plants, gave up the kitchen-garden in despair.

Juliette took it all very cheerfully, and even tried to make out that the sudden termination of business was to their advantage.

"You know, François," she said, looking up at the empty windows, "Madame's sitting-room will make such a beautiful nursery for little Virginie; it is so light and airy. And the garden has got on so much better by itself. The apple-tree has blossomed wonderfully since you left off trying to graft pears on to it; and the gooseberry bushes are really beginning to bear fruit, now you let them grow naturally. It does n't do to experiment with things too much."

They struggled along, somehow, for half-a-dozen years after that, and managed to get a good deal of happiness out of their life, though it was not

"THE GARDEN HAS GOT ON SO MUCH BETTER BY ITSELF."

quite Arcadian. François gave lessons
in painting and drawing at the schools
in St. Servans, for he had a talent for
art, and had spent many of his courting
days sketching Juliette in the orchard
or dairy. Those little pictures he sold
now, not without a heartache; but one
must live somehow, and he still had the
original. Once or twice old Petit came
over from Normandy, and made a
summer boarder of himself. At these
periods the garden sprang into vegetables and fruit as if by magic; and if the
kind old man could not find a market
for the produce, he bought it himself
and made a present of it to Juliette.

All these years they had not heard
from the angry old Count, and François,
who inherited the De Laurienne pride,
among other estimable qualities, had
never been near the Château, nor asked

for help, even in his greatest need.
They heard of M. le Comte from Petit,
who was no longer honored with
the Château custom, and did not want
it. The old nobleman, who had grown
harder and prouder than ever, lived on
at Laurienne in solitary grandeur, and
never mentioned his son to any one ;
but Petit thought his health was breaking
up, and that the lonely, loveless life was
wearing his heart away.

"Ah ! le pauvre grandpère ! " murmured Juliette, smoothing little Virginie's soft hair ; " What a dull, cold
life for him, my François ! After all,
we are richer than he ; we have our
laughter and our tears, but there are
three to laugh and cry, and the *bon*
papa to pet us all !"

It was about this time that François
won the favor of an eminent designer,

under whom he had given lessons at
the School of Art, and he obtained
well-paid commissions.   His designs
were bold and original, and pleased the
firm for whom they were undertaken,
so he was entrusted with many of their
orders, and began to make a name for
himself.   Later on he was taken on
as travelling partner, and though this
entailed long and frequent absence
from home, Juliette was too glad of his
success to demur.

When Virginie was thirteen, another
little maiden appeared at " Les Lauriers,"
and Madame's sitting-room was once
again turned into a nursery, and Virginie
installed as nurse.   Old Petit was growing infirm, and could no longer take
such long journeys, even to see his
little new granddaughter; but from time
to time they received a big hamper,

filled with good things from dairy and
orchard, accompanied by a letter in
faint, cramped writing, stiffly worded
and curiously spelt.

When little Marie Juliette could
totter about among the roses and prattle
to "maman" in newly learnt
words, they heard from
Petit that M. le
Comte was dead.
Heard too, that
his will, dated
from that au-
tumn day on
which father and son had parted, bore
no mention ·of François.   Everything
had been left to the daughter of the rich
baron, the fine cousin whom François
ought to have married.   That she had
long since become La Baronne de Val-
mency, and did not need it, only made

the will seem more unjust; it did not alter it.

François was furious. He did not believe it; so he wrote to the executors, — there was a later will he was sure. It was impossible that an old quarrel should so influence his father that after all these years he should be left with absolutely nothing.

" Oh, no," replied the executors, pleasantly, "there was certainly something." On his death-bed the old Count had murmured uneasily of " old times," and " François." Going to his side they had asked : what was his wish? The shadow of death was already upon him; he moved his head and tried to speak, but it was too late.

" François — the Blue Dragon —" was all they heard.   .

The Blue Dragon, therefore, was carefully packed and despatched with mock ceremony, and the executor's compliments, to St. Servans. "They supposed it was an heirloom; it was very handsome. Oh, yes, that was certainly something!"

Poor François was terribly angry, and not a little hurt. The porter left the Blue Dragon at the gate; and the new owner would not touch it, nor allow it to be taken up to the house. Juliette shed a few pitiful tears over the lonely old man's memory, as she took away the wrappings of the fierce-eyed monster; but her husband only regarded it with angry contempt. "If it were stolen," he said, "so much the better. It was an insult, and a laughing-stock. Let it go."

But it never was stolen, any more than the stone, vases on the gate-posts; and by-and-by the grass and weeds grew about it, and the pumpkin-vine enwreathed it, and passers-by looked upon it as some new-fashioned garden ornament. In spite of these indignities, the Blue Dragon held up his head and glared as fiercely as ever. They might leave him to the mercy of sun and rain; but all the same he had sat in a count's drawing-room, and he was the gift of a duke.

The only person to whom his arrival afforded any consolation was Marie Juliette. In some childish illness Virginie had read to her, over and over, a book of fairy tales, and these had fastened upon her baby brain in a manner peculiar to the De Lauriennes, who when once they had got an idea into their heads could never get it out.

Henceforth the little maid lived in a world of her own. She was no

longer Marie Juliette de Laurienne, she
was an Enchanted Princess, and " Les
Lauriers" was an Enchanted Castle.
No longer were her parents " papa" and
" maman,' they were the King and
Queen deprived of their lawful dignity
by the same spell which made her an
Enchanted Princess, and constituted
the Dragon her keeper.

Virginie had escaped the transform-
ing process, partly perhaps because she
was too thoroughly and indispensably
a part of the little maiden's every-day
life to be any one else than Virginie,
and partly because as nurse and teacher
her duties often made it necessary to
break into the day-dream in which her
charge was absorbed.

" It is time for bed, Juliette," or
" Come and get ready for tea," were
words which broke the spell of fairyland

and obliged the Princess to bid farewell
to her faithful Dragon, and submit to
the indignities of evening bath or brush
and comb.

But nothing struck such blank despair into the heart of the royal maiden
as the summons to lessons.

When she heard the clear call echo-
ing down the laurel-walk: "Aux leçons, leçons, ma Marie Juliette!" the
Princess would whisper a sad adieu in
the ear of her dear Blue Dragon, and
leave a tear shining on his gorgeous
head, while she walked slowly away to
meet Virginie's coaxing face, and the
big brown A B C book with its moral
stories and long, thin lines of spelling.

Once free from the influence of " La
Fille Diligente." or " Le Méchant Gar-
çon," the Princess would fly to her
monster and spend hours beside him,

with the book of fairy tales on her knee,
and her fingers wreathing flowers for
his adornment.

" Beauty and the Beast," her father
called them ; and very often a friendly
pupil, walking home with him in the
evening, would pause to sketch the
pair, while François looked on or gave
a helping hand.

" What do you do all day, Beauty ? "
asked one kind student who had given
her his sketch. " Don't you find it dull
down here by the gate ? "

" I watch for the King," answered
the Princess, with grave condescension,
" and for travellers who have lost their
way looking for the Tree of Life. I
keep the key, and the Dragon guards
the gate. No one can enter if I am not
here, for he would devour them."

When the winter came, the Princess

did not desert her post, though she could no longer sit among the pumpkin-leaves. She was allowed to run up and down the laurel-walk with her little hoop or her skipping rope, and when the snow came she built a beautiful white castle round the Dragon, and snowballed him till the walls fell in. Even on wet days the King carried her down, wrapped in his great-coat, to kiss her hand to the china monster.

So the poor Blue Dragon, though neglected and despised by every one else, had opened up a beautiful world for little Marie Juliette, — a world in which she lived as happy as the day was long.

But no one need be surprised at that; for was he not the gift of a duke?

CHAPTER IV.

UNDER THE TREE OF LIFE.

BEFORE the Apples of Life had turned to gold, the traveller came again to the Enchanted Castle. He came to return the Princess's little handkerchief, the one in which she had bound up his hand when he tore it getting through the sweetbrier hedge.

The Princess was at the gate as usual, singing to the Dragon in a clear, shrill treble.

"Petite Bo Boutons
A perdu ses moutons — "

But when she saw the traveller at the gate, she broke off her song, and ran to let him in.

"Why have you come so soon?" she called out. "The apples are not ripe yet. I said, 'When the King comes,' but it wants two weeks and four days to that."

"Yes, I remember what you told me; but I have not come for the apples. I have come to bring back your handkerchief; and here is something for you. It comes straight from fairyland."

It was a book of French fairy-tales, those charming fairly-tales of Madame d'Aulnoy, bound in red and gold, and beautifully illustrated. The Princess sat down on the gravel-walk to undo the wrappers, and gave a little scream of delight.

"Oh, how beautiful! And the pictures are painted, and the edges are gold! Oh, what a charming traveller you are! And here is something written, — what does it say?"

" ' To Mademoiselle Marie Juliette de Laurienne, from her sincere friend, Godfrey Traverse.' Is that right?"

" Oh, quite right!" said the Princess, who would not have known had it been wrong; " but who is Godfrey Traverse?"

" I am — " he began, then seeing the look of disappointment in the dark eyes raised to his, — " why! — don't you like it?"

" It is a very nice name," she said slowly, unwilling to offend him; " but — but the travellers are always called Cheri or Charmant, and then they turn out to be princes. I am sorry your name is not Charmant. I always said you were a prince in disguise; but the

Queen said there is no disguise about Englishmen; they cannot keep it up. Are you a prince in disguise?"

" No, I am afraid not," he said laughing; " the Queen is quite right."

" Then you must be a knight," said Marie Juliette, turning the leaves of her fairy-tale book; " the knights never put on disguise, they fought the Dragons, and — oh, I *do* hope you won't begin to fight the Dragon! You will never bring your sword here, will you? Please, please don't!"

" No, no, I am quite safe. I promise you I will never fight your Dragon. But how long are you going to sit in the dust?"

" It is so delightful to have a quite new fairy-book!" she cried, lifting her April face, all smiles now, as she jumped up and led his willing steps along the

laurel-walk. " The old one was Virginie's, and so many of the leaves were
loose. And there was a big hole in
the cover, where Virginie dropped it in
the grate once, while she was watching
my tisane when I was ill."

The Enchanted Castle looked much
the same as on that evening when the
traveller had first walked up to it in
the sunset light. The long, thin finger
of the sun-dial pointed to noon; and
the swallows and pigeons were evidently
taking a siesta, for only the bees hovered
lazily about the roses.

They avoided the sweetbrier hedge,
and went round the house by a little
path, overshadowed by lilac bushes,
which brought them to the back-door.
Now, as then, it stood open, and from
within came the savory smell of *pot-
au-feu*, and the suggestive clatter of

plates. As they approached, the tortoise-shell cat came leaping down the
steps, followed by an imperative "Shoo!
shoo!" and the whisk of a white apron,
and the next moment Virginie appeared in the doorway, a basin
and knife in her hand,
and her apron full
vegetables.

"Ah, it is Mon-
sieur?" she cried
brightly, putting down
the basin and knife, and giving him
her hand. "It is well, Monsieur, that
you were not on the step a little
sooner; you would have got the corner of my apron in your face, instead
of that naughty Mimi! She has been
trying to steal our dinner!"

Here the Princess interposed with
her present, which, after it had been

duly admired, she carried off to show
the Queen; and Virginie sat down on
the wooden bench, and opened her
apron, displaying a heap of amber
carrots, russet potatoes, and long French
beans.

"Will you not rest, Monsieur?" she
said, clearing a place for him; "it is
warm, although it is late in September,
and you have had a long walk."

Monsieur sat down and watched her,
as, with deft fingers, she peeled the
potatoes and threw them into the bowl.

"Can I not help you?" he asked,
feeling quite idle beside all this brisk
business, and wishing he had something
to do with his hands.

"If Monsieur likes, he may hold the
pie-dish, — so," said Virginie, adjusting
it, — "while I scrape the carrots. That
is division of labor."

"'CAN I NOT HELP YOU?' HE ASKED."

"One-sided labor, I think. Let me do that for you."

"Oh, no!" replied Virginie, shaking her head till the curls fell over her eyes and she had to push them back; "you would not do it at all nicely, and you would be so slow. Men are poor cooks."

"But your best cooks are men," objected the traveller, watching the little yellow shavings curl round her quick, sharp knife.

"Ah, yes, but they are French; you are an Englishman."

Evidently they had a poor opinion of Englishmen in the Enchanted Castle.

"And when do you start for Normandy, Monsieur?" went on Virginie. "You will perhaps get there just in time for the apple-harvest. That would be charming."

"I go to-morrow," he said; "I have settled the papers, and now I am the possessor of a little farm, and an orchard or two. I hope to get my mother there by November."

"So soon? That will be nice for you both. And you will keep her company?"

"Yes," he said, looking away into the clear blue sky, through the branches of the apple-tree; "I will stay with her, —it will not be for long."

Virginie did not speak. She followed his glance, and gazed thoughtfully at the stretch of azure flecked with tiny, white clouds. Through the noonday hush came the faint chirrup of a cricket hidden in the grass. Only that broke the silence till the traveller spoke again.

"Your little sister has promised me some of the Apples of Life," he said smiling. "It is a pretty fancy of hers; but I think for some of us they never ripen, — only hang out of reach on the tree, dazzling our eyes like the fruit of Tantalus."

"Oh, no," said Virginie, gently, "I am sure every one has a share in the harvest. Sometimes it is late."

She had taken some bean-pods into her hand and was paring them, drawing off the skin in long green threads.

"Perhaps," she said, looking up with a soft light in her eyes, "your mother is going to gather her harvest, Monsieur, in the Garden of Paradise."

"Perhaps," he said more hopefully, "thank you, Mademoiselle Virginie."

"There, I have finished. Merci, Monsieur! Now we will go to the mother; she will be pleased to see you."

They went into the big, airy kitchen,
— the traveller supposed it was a kitchen
because there was a little army of sauce-
pans on the fire, and a tall dresser stood
opposite, laden with blue and white
china. Virginie threw her vegetables
into the largest saucepan, and went to
another door, calling to her mother to
come and see " Monsieur l'Anglais."

Madame came running from some-
where upstairs, with a feather-broom in
her hand, and a duster over her arm.
She welcomed " Monsieur l'Anglais "
with effusion, and asked him to stay to
lunch, — an invitation which Marie Juliette imperatively echoed.

" You must stay, my knight ! " she
cried, pulling him toward the table.
"See ! I have set a place for you ; and
there is Mimi, keeping your chair. You
must stay ! "

" Tais toi, Mariette ! " cried Madame,
" Be more polite, and do not say ' must '!
It is for Monsieur to decide ; and per-
haps he does not like *pot-au-feu ?* "

The traveller looked at Virginie, as
though doubtful of the etiquette observed
in an Enchanted Castle. She was cut-
ting a long loaf, using the broad window-sill as a sideboard, and paused to
divide the crust before she looked up
with a smile.

" Stay, Monsieur," she said, " and
help to eat the vegetables, as you helped
to prepare them."

So Monsieur stayed, and felt himself
drawn deeper and deeper into the spell
of enchantment every moment. He
thought he had never tasted anything
half so delicious as the homely bouillon,
which the Queen served out of an
earthenware bowl ; perhaps it was be-

cause he had helped Virginie prepare
it, — at least, so she said, though he had
only held the pie-dish. As for the
sweet cider brought out in his honor,
he could never remember such a flavor
in the old port at home; and the brown
bread and honey which Virginie put on
his plate, might have been ambrosia
served by a French Hebe.

But everything must have an end,
even in an Enchanted Castle, and the
traveller sat in the window-seat and
read fairy-tales to the Princess, while
Virginie cleared away and washed up
the dishes. He was glad that Madame
kept up a running accompaniment of
small-talk while she moved to and fro,
for his pronunciation was not Parisian,
and the Princess was continually cor-
recting it, pointing out his faults with
alarming candor.

In the midst of " La Chatte Blanche," Mimi leaped suddenly onto the sill, and put a soft paw right across the page ; and as she refused to go away, the reading came to an end, much to the relief of the poor traveller.

" Monsieur Traverse," said Madame, coming up with a pretty pleading in her eyes, and clasped hands, ;" Virginie tells me you start for my country to-morrow. Ah, if Monsieur would deliver a little remembrance to the *bon* papa for me ! A winter wrap I have made, and some of Virginie's honey, — so good for the cough from which he suffers ! I wish so much to send a little token, and I cannot afford the post."

She made her request, and the innocent avowal of their poverty, so simply and frankly, that Monsieur felt ready to do anything in his power, and promised

6

to deliver any number of messages and souvenirs.

" Ah, but he was too good! I will write a letter, and perhaps Monsieur would stay to tea? That would give her so much pleasure, and the little parcel should be quite ready by then."

Monsieur accepted with pleasure, and Madame, after bidding Virginie entertain their guest, went upstairs to pour out her love and anxiety to the good old father whose health was failing.

" Come out," said the Princess, climbing down from the window-seat with Mimi in her arms, " let us go and sit under the Tree of Life, and count the apples that are nearly ripe. Come then, Virginie will be ready soon, and then she will bring her sewing out there, — won't you, Virginie?"

" But, yes — I will join you!"

said Virginie, brightly, "only Marie Juliette must not fatigue Monsieur Traverse to read any more. It is hard for him, the French language; that I can see."

Monsieur Traverse laughed, and followed the Princess out and across the lawn to the apple-tree. He lifted her onto a moss-grown branch, "So high," the little maiden said, "I can almost catch the clouds that come sailing down to look through the branches." But Mimi went up even higher, and sat far out of reach, watching the swallows.

Presently Virginie came out with her sewing, some light-checked print she was making into shirts for the King, — so the Princess volunteered, — and sat on a lower branch with her cotton and scissors in her lap, while the traveller lay in the long grass beneath and looked up at them.

"We are out of your reach!" laughed little Marie Juliette, clapping her hands, and peeping down from her leafy bower. "Mimi and Virginie and I! We are three princesses, and we sit up here with the Golden Apples, out of your reach!"

"Yes, you are out of my reach," he said, laughing back; but he sighed too.

"But you can climb," said the Princess, as though in challenge. "The Prince had to climb, you know, before he got the apples; but first there was the golden ring."

"And what did he do with the ring?" asked the traveller, gently waving a faded leaf to and fro to keep off the tiny gnats, who were holding a carnival down there in the grass.

"He gave it to the Princess — oh! Mimi! Look out for yourself! — Mimi is coming!"

Mimi leaped skilfully from one bough to another, and down into the soft grass with a spring, for her quick eyes had caught the moving leaf, and she pounced upon it at once.

"There is one Princess for you!" cried Marie Juliette. "But we will not come down, Virginie and I. You must climb for us and for the Golden Apples too."

But the traveller did not climb. He looked at Virginie's face, bent over her work, with the shadows of the leaves dancing on her hair, and playing about her dress. He was wondering why she was so silent.

"How dull you are!" cried the Princess, from her perch above. "You are

a knight,—tell us about your adventures.
How many maidens have you rescued ? "

" None at all," said the knight; " but
I have lived in a country far away, and
seen giant forests, and birds of red-and-
gold.   Shall I tell you about those ? "

" Yes, do !   Lift me down, so that I
may hear you ; but don't crumple Virginie's work."

So he lifted her down and sat her in
the grass beside him, with Mimi in her
lap, while he told tales of Australian
life, in the best French he could muster.
The Princess corrected his mistakes,
and Virginie listened as she sewed.

When they had exhausted the won-
ders of Australia, he told them another
story.   Rather a sad story of the terrible tropical fever, and of a happy family
that had grown very small now, and of
two travellers who came over the sea to

England, and of one traveller who was dying.

" Mais que c'est triste!" sighed the Princess, when this story ended. She was sorry it was so sad; she liked better to hear about the fields where one picked up gold, and the forests full of beautiful birds. But I think Virginie thought the other story the most interesting, though she did not say so. She only looked thoughtfully up at the little white clouds for a moment, with her hands clasped over the checked shirt; and then she stood up and gathered her work together.

" It is nearly tea-time," she said. " Will Monsieur excuse me while I set the table?"

And without waiting for an answer, she went into the house.

Madame was there in a little flutter

of excitement, when the Princess and
her friend made their appearance at the
tea-table. She had her little gifts and
the long letter quite ready, and had many
directions to give, as to the whereabouts
of the farm, and the habits of the
farmer, and also a little word of intro-
duction for the benefit of Monsieur
l'Anglais, to whom she hoped the *bon*
papa might be of service.

"For he is of great experience, and
could advise well concerning this little
property, — as Monsieur might be taken
in, if left to himself."

Monsieur, secretly amused at the idea
of a barrister being taken in by a few
French peasants, thanked her politely,
put the letter into his pocket, and
turned his attention to the excellent
coffee and hot meal-cakes, which Madame dispensed as she talked.   The

Princess, perched upon her high-chair,
and Virginie, who sat opposite, kept up
a brisk fire of laughing chatter, and
between them the traveller felt quite
boyish, and even ventured on
a few jokes of his own, deliv-
ered in such ludicrously bad
French that Marie Juliette
shrieked with delight, and
even Madame, though
distressed at such a want of
courtesy, could not help a smile.

"Monsieur will improve," said Virginie, laughingly, as she sugared his
coffee, "when he finds himself with
strangers on this journey. But I think,
among the bourgeoisie at least, he had
better not venture on jokes. It might
be — embarrassing."

Later on, with Madame's gifts in his
hands, her letter in his pocket, and her

kindly farewell ringing in his ears, the
traveller left the Enchanted Castle and
once again walked down to the gate,
escorted by Virginie and the Princess.
There sat the Blue Dragon in a fiery
glow of sunset radiance, encircled by
the hairy arms of the pumpkin-vine.
The Princess thought he glared at the
traveller more fiercely than ever, or
was it the red sun shining in his
eyes?

"Good-by, my knight," she said, holding open the gate for him to pass out,
"tell us, when you come back, if you
have rescued any distressed maidens
on the road to Normandy."

"Ah, yes, Monsieur Traverse," said
Virginie, holding out her hand, "you
will come and see us again, will you
not? Just to tell us of your little home,
and how you find *le bon grandpère.*"

" I should be only too glad ! " replied
the traveller, trying to manipulate the
parcels so as to take off his hat and
shake hands without letting them fall
into the road. " I cannot thank you
enough for having made my stay here
so — "

" Mais, non ! " laughed Virginie, "you
really cannot thank us — so do not
try. Look to your French, Monsieur,
and when you return we will have
some more — how do you say —
reedles."

He was in the road now, had turned
to go, and looked back as he heard the
iron gate snap to, and the key grate in
the rusty lock. There was the Princess
on tip-toe, laughing through the bars,
and beside her, tall enough to catch the
rosy sunset-flush on her face and on
the soft folds of her muslin scarf, stood

Virginie. Behind them both sat the Dragon, with outstretched wings.

"Adieu!" cried Virginie, waving her scarf, and "Adieu!" the Princess echoed.

"Adieu!" said the traveller, baring his head; and then he walked slowly along the lane, and out of sight of the Enchanted Castle.

CHAPTER V.

HOW THEY FOUND THE TREASURE THAT WAS GUARDED BY THE DRAGON.

HE storm has not broken the Tree of Life!" cried the Princess, joyously, " it only looks more beautiful still, all wet and shining, and I can see the Golden Apples through the leaves! Ah, *cher* papa! may I not go out and gather one, to see if they are quite ripe?"

She sat in the window-seat, looking out onto the wind-swept garden, fresh

and green and wet after the storm of
last night, — one of those late thunder-
storms that come at the end of September, as though summer were leaving in
a burst of tears, after lingering as long
as she could to be at last driven out
by scolding autumn.

The wind-shaken fruit-trees rustled
gently in the clear morning air, shaking
down a shower of rain-drops with every
little breeze; the grass was strewn with
a gorgeous mosaic of fallen leaves, —
scarlet and gold and bronze, — with here
and there a russet pear, or a ripe, green
fig, and the apple-tree stood in the
midst, showing through a thin veil of
glowing leaves its wealth of ruddy
gold.

The Princess laughed with delight
as she caught sight of the ripe fruit,
from her seat in the window. Had

they not put on their golden dress to
welcome the King? — the King who
had come home last night, all through
the cold and the rain. She turned a
pleading face to François, and climbing
down from the sill, ran to clasp her
hands about his arm and pulled him to
the door.

"Say it then! Ah, say I may run
out to see if the apples are quite ripe!
For you know — the traveller comes
to-morrow!"

François looked down at the wet
grass, and up at the wet trees, and then
into his little daughter's face.

"No, mignonne, see the grass is
soaked with rain. This afternoon, perhaps, it will have dried up, for the sun
is shining now, — but not this morning,
petite."

The Princess sighed, and looked up

with wistful eyes at the swallows dart-
ing to and fro against the clear blue of
the autumn sky. Happy swallows!
They need not stay at home this lovely
morning, because the grass was wet;
ah, if she had but wings like theirs,
and could float and flutter in the
sunshine!

But she laughed the next moment,
for there was poor Mimi, mewing dis-
tressfully as she picked her way daintily
through the long grass, lifting first one
wet paw and then the other, and shaking the rain-drops from her whiskers
in evident disgust. Mimi and the
Princess were companions in misfortune; they would go indoors together
till the world outside was dry.

"Bien, mignonne!" said François, as
she turned, still laughing, and stepped
across the threshold, followed by Mimi.

"Come and see my sketches, and I will tell you stories of the fisher-girls of Boulogne, and of the pretty boutonnières one meets in Paris; and when you are tired of pictures, we will read some of that wonderful fairy-book of yours — eh?"

"Mais, oui! ça sera charmant!" cried the Princess, clapping her hands; and soon she was deep in the delights of her father's big sketchbook. Mimi and the wet garden, and even the Apples of Life, for the time forgotten.

But only for the time. When dinner was over, and François sat in the window peeling a fig for her especial benefit, Marie Juliette renewed her entreaties,

7

" Just to go and look at the Golden
Apples! See how the sun shines, and
the grass does not look so very wet,
and you can carry me to the apple-
tree! Ah, yes, Papa!"

Her persuasions at length prevailed,
and François lifted her to his shoulder
and carried her across the lawn to the
Tree of Life. Ah, happy Princess!
How smooth and yellow shone the
apples, how sweet they smelled! How
the birds sang, and the sunlight danced
on the leaves, and the swallows shot
past like silver arrows, and the white
pigeons cooed in the sun! All the
world was rejoicing because the Golden
Apples were ripe ; but the Blue Dragon did not know yet. Quick as
thought, she freed herself from the
supporting arm and wriggled to the
ground.

"Ah, my poor Dragon! He is left out in the cold; he does not know. He has guarded the Apples of Life, oh, so long and so patiently, and now they are ripe, and I must tell him, mon cher! I must! I will run down the laurel-walk where the gravel dries so quickly, you know. I shall not get my shoes wet; let me go to the dear Blue Dragon!"

"Méchante!" laughed François; but he did not demur, and watched the little figure flit round the house, and dart through the hedge of sweetbrier.

The Princess ran on down the drive; the rose-bushes, beaten down by the rain, hung wet and sweet-scented over the path, and the gravel was strewn with crimson petals. All the garden was a world of flowers and sunlight and song, and the Princess sang the sweetest of all, in a clear, little treble, pushing back the rose sprays, as she danced along.

> " À mon beau château,
> L'on y danse, l'on y danse !
> Et moi, je suis la plus gaie,
> La plus gaie fillette en France ! "

How glad the Blue Dragon would be! She would deck him with roses, and

then the passers-by would know what a good Dragon he had been, and would stop to admire him. So she filled the skirt of her little green gown with the fresh, damp blossoms and hastened on.

> " À mon beau château,
> L'on y chante, l'on y chante !

'Chantons ! dansons ! la vie
Est tout à fait charmante ! '
Tra, la, la ! tra, la, la ! "

Ah, happy Princess !

Down the laurel-walk where the birds
were singing, through the tangled thicket
of the pumpkin-vine, and then, —

Alas, for the Princess ! Alas, for the
Blue Dragon !

Under a heap of stone fragments,
battered and broken, he lay — headless !
The storm that had passed harmless
over the Tree of Life, had killed the
Blue Dragon. The wild wind of last
night had blown down one of the old
stone vases from the gateway right
onto the poor china monster, and there
they both lay in ruins among the pumpkin-leaves.

The Princess stood for a moment
gazing with wide-open eyes upon the
scene of destruction. It seemed too ter-

rible to believe! Then she plunged
into the long, wet grass and threw herself down beside the body of the poor
Dragon in a storm of grief. The roses
fell from her gown and lay on the
ground forgotten; the birds in the
laurel-walk seemed to sing no longer,
only to cut the clear air with shrill
cries, and a cloud blew up out of the
west and hid the sun. But these
changes did not surprise the Princess,
they seemed rather in keeping with her
sorrow, and she felt that earth and sky
were mourning with her for the poor
Blue Dragon.

So she lay there, prone upon the wet
grass in the shadow of a broken wing,
and gave herself up to her passionate
grief. All the beautiful romance of
fairy life seemed shut out from her
experience. The Dragon had opened

the gates of fairyland, and now he was dead. She was no longer a Princess; her home was no longer an Enchanted Castle; the Tree of Life with its Golden Apples seemed but a poor pretence. The gold and the glitter had faded from everything; she was now only a lonely little girl in a very sad world, and the magician who had conjured up that old, delightful dream was but a blue china monster with a broken head.

"Where is the Princess, mon père?" cried Virginie, coming from the fire with the coffee-pot in her hands, as François walked into the kitchen at tea-time.

"The Princess? Why, — isn't she here? Then she must be upstairs with that Mimi of hers. Call her."

" But, no ; she is not in the house. I
thought you had been for a walk
together."

" Where have your eyes been, little
maid ? I have been sitting on the
bench under the window the whole
afternoon, reading ' Le Figaro,' and yes,
— I will confess, — I have been dozing
too."

" And Marie Juliette ? "

" Oh, now I remember. She ran to
see her dear monster, only for a moment. Surely she is returned long ago,
with Mimi as I tell you."

" Mais, non, here is Mimi. The Princess must be still in the garden — ah,
quel dommage ! and she with her little
thin shoes ! Run, cher papa, and call
her in to tea."

François pocketed his paper, and
walked leisurely out of the house and

"LYING FAST ASLEEP BESIDE HER FALLEN IDOL."

down the garden, still occupied with an
art criticism in " Le Figaro," and not
thinking much about the Princess, till
he came upon her suddenly, lying fast
asleep beside her fallen idol.

"Mon Dieu!" he cried with a start,
"asleep in the wet grass, — and all this
time! Peste! what a fool I have been!"

He strode through the pumpkin-
leaves and stooped to wake her. Even
in his anxiety the love of art came
uppermost, and he paused a moment
to admire the pretty picture, — the
sleeping figure of the little Princess
with the fallen roses massed in rich
clusters against her faded green gown,
her curly head thrown back against the
wing of the blue monster, whose turquoise coloring lent sharp relief to the
warm coloring of an oval cheek, still
wet with tears.

"Tragedy and comedy," he muttered, smiling; and then he bent down and shook her gently.

"Wake, mignonne! wake, cherette, and come to tea. Ah, how cold and wet my pretty bird is!"

The Princess opened her eyes with a half sob, and looked at him blankly. He raised her gently, and gave a glance at the headless body of the poor Blue Dragon. From the broken neck a corner of white paper projected; François pulled it out and opened a folded sheet, glancing carelessly down the page. The next moment he startled the Princess by calling out:—

"The will! Grand Dieu, the will!"

The words were as Greek to Marie Juliette, and when he caught her in his arms and strode up the drive, kissing and fondling her with broken exclamations of joy and hope, she received his caresses in wondering silence. She was but half awake; the shadow of her loss loomed vaguely through the dream-world from which she was not wholly yet returned, still the shadow was there, growing more distinct each moment. And how could the King laugh and be so glad, while she lay in his arms, with a great sorrow at her heart and big, bitter tears on her lashes? As she dreamily wondered, they crossed the lawn, they were at the house, and there was *maman* to meet them.

"Ah, pauvrette! She will have taken cold, I fear," began Madame, anxiously; but François cut her short by crying joyously, —

"The will, my Juliette, the will!"

"Hé, quoi!" cried Madame. "Whose will? What will? Where?"

" *His* will ! — mon père — the Blue
Dragon ! " shouted De Laurienne ; " and
it is *I*, my Juliette, who am the heir, — it is
mine, the château ! Voilà the true will ! "

Madame stood still on the doorstep,
eyes and mouth wide open in surprise,
half doubting her senses, half fearing for
his. Was this a " poisson d'Avril ? "
No, it could not be ; they were in sedate
September yet, — then her face fell in
pitying compassion.

" Hush, my poor François ; it is the
old will, it is of no use whatever."

" Bah ! Is it that you are deaf, Juliette ;
and that I am not a man to know what
I am about ? It is the latest will of all,
— the *true* will ! "

" Vrai-ment ? " asked Madame, with
cautious hesitation.

" Parbleu ! " cried François, impatiently, " Suis-je fou ? " Then he flung

an arm round the Queen's waist, and kissed her on both cheeks, " Vraiment, little wife! See — the day, the month, the year, — before he died he repented after all!"

" The saints be praised for that!" said Madame, devoutly.

" Amen!" cried Monsieur, laughing.

" But where — how did you get it, mon ami? Is it that they have written, — those lawyers from Laurienne?"

" No, no; but I understand — I see it all now. Ah, the poor father! Do you remember what he said when he was dying? 'François — the Blue Dragon — ' I see it now."

" But I do not. Tell me, quick, François! I die of curiosity!"

" Why, the Blue Dragon is broken; the storm, you know — and stuffed down his throat — hidden away — was this!"

A wail of anguish startled them. The Princess, who had slipped to the ground, had been listening quietly; but the last words made clear that dull pain at her heart, and published abroad the cause of her sorrow. With a burst of tears she snatched at the paper held loosely in Madame's fingers, and flinging it to the ground, trampled upon it with passionate cries.

"Ah, le vilain! Mais que c'est méchant — cruel! Ah, le pauvre Dragon Bleu! Il lui a fait mourir!"

"Tais-toi, Juliette!" cried François, angrily, "see what you are doing! Stop — and take your naughty feet away!"

But the cry of baby despair went straight to Madame's heart, — even a Queen may be a mother, and have a mother's tender heart, — and she held out her arms, with loving words of sympathy.

The Princess paused in her malicious little dance, and looked up, with one small foot still raised, the other set firmly on the crumpled paper.

"Come then, my Marie Juliette!" coaxed Madame, "Mother understands and is sorry! Mother knows all about it!"

But Marie Juliette shook her head sadly, and brought down her foot in a final stamp, that left a stain of wet, green grass on the last clause of the will.

"No," she said with a little sob, "you *cannot* understand. You never had a Dragon!"

And with a pathetic air of sad superiority, she walked quietly into the house.

8

CHAPTER VI.

HOW THE PRINCESS MOURNED THE FALLEN DRAGON.

"BUT we are poor," said François, gloomily, as they sat at tea a little later, "who will undertake the suit for us? The Baron is avaricious; La Baronne will dispute our claim; and those sly foxes, the Laurienne lawyers, are too cunning to bite off their own heads! We have rank and wealth and crafty tongues against us."

" N'importe ! " responded Madame, cheerily, " the right is on our side."

" Pah, that goes for so much ! " cried François, with a shrug and a snap of his fingers. " Might against right ; you know who goes into the corner."

" But if we have the will, they cannot prove — "

" Oh, a lawyer can prove anything ! " said François.

" Bien ! " cried Virginie, clapping her hands, and looking up with a bright, flushed face, " there is Monsieur Traverse, he is a lawyer ; he is our friend ; he will plead for us ! Voilà tout ! "

" And who is this Traverse ? "

" A Monsieur anglais — the young lawyer — " began Madame ; but the Princess, who had been quietly eating her *soupe-au-lait*, interposed.

" He is not a lawyer," she said ; " he is a knight."

"So!" cried her father, laughing, " if we are to have a knight to fight our battles, all is sure to go well! He will enter the lists with a flourish of trumpets, and throw down his glove, like the brave knights of old. And with his good sword he will rescue the Princess, win back the castle, and slay the fierce Dragon!"

The smiles that had crept into Marie Juliette's wide eyes, and dimpled her cheeks, died away, and a rush of tears came in their stead.

"The Dragon is dead!" she said with a catch in her voice and a brave endeavor to keep back the tears. She bent her head over her basin of bread and milk, and stared hard at the blue Chinaman walking up the side. But two drops trembled on her lashes, and fell into the bowl, and slid down the

Chinaman's pigtail into the milk. They were very salt tears; but the Princess did not pause till she had emptied the basin, and then she looked up with a little forced smile.

"May I get down! *Please* let me go and call Mimi!"

Madame knew that Mimi was purring cosily under the table; but she had seen the struggle, and was pitiful. So she nodded, and the Princess folded her hands, and bent her curly head.

"Nous vous rendons grâces de tous vos bienfaits, O Dieu — ainsi soit-il," she said, in rather a hurry, and scrambled down from her high-chair, and out of the room. She climbed the stairs, holding her breath all the while to keep back the sobs. She was proud; she would not let them see her crying any more. She felt hot and ashamed

that they had seen so much already.
How could they know, how could they
understand all that the Blue Dragon
had been to her? The King despised
it; the Queen scarcely thought of it;
Virginie — oh, yes! — Virginie thought
it was a very good thing, because it

amused the Prin-
cess, — that was all.
But to her — oh, what the
Blue Dragon had been to her!
When she had gained the nursery,
the Princess knelt down by the low window-seat, laid her head on the broad
ledge, and gave full vent to her grief.
She did not notice the tiny pink roses
that thrust their pretty, inquisitive faces
round the lattice, and shook a few
sympathetic drops upon her curls; she

did not hear the busy murmur of the
bronze bees, nor look up when the
swallows flashed past, with a sharp
quiver of silver-lined wings. It was
not till something soft and warm rubbed
against her cheek that she raised her
streaming eyes, and saw, through a mist
of tears, a blurred picture of poor Mimi,
walking round and round upon the
sill.

"Oh, Mimi!" she cried sadly. " It
is never, never, that you will be a beautiful princess, like ' La Chatte Blanche '
— now. My pretty Mimi, I am so sorry
for you! You must always be a poor
little cat!"

Mimi arched her back, and rubbed
her nose against her little mistress's
shoulder, and purred louder than ever.
Perhaps she was thinking complacently
of the mice that a princess could

never enjoy ; perhaps she had designs
upon the swallows. But Marie Juliette
thought she was trying to make the best
of things, and patted her approvingly.

"You are very brave, my Mimi, I
wish I could be brave!" she sighed,
and just then she heard steps upon the
stairs. Some one else had followed
Mimi, and was close to the nursery
door. The Princess climbed up onto
the window-sill in a violent hurry, and
began talking to her pet, very fast, and
pointing down to the white pigeons in
the garden.

The Queen came in, with Virginie
behind her, and went over to the
window.

"What, sitting in a draught!" she
cried, "and such hot cheeks and hands
— ah, I fear it is a bad cold that you
have taken, mignonne. all out in the

wet grass! My love must go to bed, or she will be ill."

The Princess winked away a tell-tale tear, and stroked Mimi's fur assiduously. She submitted to the verdict of bed, and to the glass of orange water that Madame administered as a soothing draught, without a word. In silence she allowed herself to be undressed and put into her little white cot, by Virginie, who, smiling, bent to wish her a loving good-night.

"Sweet sleep and pleasant dreams ma Marie Juliette!" she said, with a kiss, and then she moved quietly about the room, folding little clothes, and drawing the white curtains across the lattice.

The Princess lay quite still till Virginie had gone downstairs, and then she cried herself to sleep.

The morrow had decked itself out most charmingly, in blue and white, and smiles and sunshine. The morning breeze had kissed away all the tears of yesterday, and set the leaves a-quiver with delight, and the butterflies a-dancing to the music of the bees. And now it was late in the afternoon, and the breeze had fallen asleep, tired out with play, so that the rustling boughs no longer stirred the silence with leafy whispers, and the butterflies left off dancing and rested, perched among rose-leaves, or poised on the lavender spikes. Only the bees went on with their low, monotonous chorus, "Coming, come, come, com-ing!"

And the traveller was coming along the lane humming a tune, with a flower in his buttonhole. He was happy, though he could not have told you why. Perhaps it was the sunshine, — or was it his new coat? Perhaps — but that was a secret that only his own heart guessed at; it was certainly not to be trusted to the bees or the roses, for they would tell the butterflies, and there is no keeping a secret with the butterflies, — the whole garden would know what was going on in less than no time.

So he passed them all by and made for the path under the lilacs. It would never do to spoil his "get up" by a scrimmage with the sweetbrier hedge. But as he crossed the lawn he heard a low murmur in the porch that could hardly come from the bees; it was a tone too high, and there was the pretty music of the French accent. The traveller listened and became more convinced, for the words he heard were set

to the tune of an old French song.
He stepped a little nearer and listened
more intently. Through the tangle of
roses that clung about the porch came
the murmur more distinctly, with the
musical rise and fall of a girlish voice.

> " Si vous n'avez rien à me dire,
>   Pourquoi venir auprès de moi ? "

He looked through the roses and saw
the pink tip of an ear veiled in tendrils
of dusky hair, and the soft contour of
a cheek and chin. A blossom-dusted
bee bounced out of a rose and buzzed
about his face, as though resenting the
intrusion, and he turned and made silent war against it with his pocket-hand-
kerchief. Having routed the enemy, he
stole once more to the lattice-work of
leaf and flower, and listened with a
smile. The pretty voice had wandered

now into the cooing sing-song of a
lullaby.

> " Do, do, bébé, do !
> L'enfant dormira tantôt ! "

" This is too bad ! " thought the traveller, waking to the fact that his eaves-
dropping might, perhaps, seem hardly
fair to the unconscious singer. He
brushed the leaves from his coat, and
went quickly round to the front of the
porch.

There sat Virginie with the Princess
in her arms, gently rocking to and fro,
her fingers busy with some knitting,
while with one foot she kept time to
the low music of her lullaby. The
book of fairy-stories had fallen to the
ground, and lay open in the sunshine
with an earwig slowly crawling up the
white margin. A shadow fell across
the page, and Virginie looked up with

a little flush of surprise and a smile of welcome.

"Hush!" she said softly, with a finger on her lip; "the Princess is not well. She is so drowsy, and her cheeks are so hot, I am afraid she is going to be ill."

"The Princess ill!" echoed the traveller. "Oh, that cannot be! She is tired perhaps with playing in the sun."

"Ah, no, she has not played at all to-day. She has been fretting for the Blue Dragon," said Virginie; and she told him of the broken plaything, and of the finding of the will. He listened gravely, leaning against the porch with his eyes fixed on the small black earwig travelling across the sunny page. Virginie wondered why he did not congratulate them, and said so.

"Oh, yes; I am glad," said the trav-

eller, " it is great good fortune, Mademoiselle, for you."

But he thought that it was not at all
good fortune for himself, he felt even
sorry; and then he looked up peni-
tently, and held out his hand.

" How selfish I am!" he said cheerfully, " a thousand congratulations,
Mademoiselle! I am very glad for all
your sakes."

He felt proud of himself after this
little speech, and hoped that Virginie
would notice the improvement in his
French. But she was looking anxiously at the Princess.

" Pauvre petite!" she said softly.
" Feel, Monsieur, how hot her forehead
is."

She took his hand and laid it on the
little white brow under the tumbled curls.

" Yes;" said Monsieur, then gently

touching with his finger the flushed
cheek that rested on Virginie's shoulder,
" I am afraid it is a bad chill, I think
I should take her in, Mademoiselle."

"Yes; perhaps you are right," Virginie said, as she unclasped the hot
hands from her neck and prepared to
rise.

But the traveller bent down quickly,
and took the Princess into his arms, saying, "Hush, hush!" as gently as a woman.
Virginie picked up the fairy-tale book,
shaking the earwig from its leaves, and
led the way round by the lilac-shadowed
path.

" I do not think we will attempt the
sweetbrier hedge this time. Eh, Monsieur?" she said, looking back over her
shoulder, with a gleam of roguish laughter in her eyes. And the traveller
shook his head, laughing quietly, for

he was afraid of disturbing the Princess. The little cheek close to his was
hot as fire, and the breath came quick
and short through the dry, parted lips.
He stepped so carefully that his charge
was still asleep when they reached the
kitchen, and Virginie held up a finger
of warning to Madame, who met them
with outstretched hands, and words of
welcome. Her bright face grew anxious as the trio entered, and François,
too, came forward with an air of
concern.

"Oh, it is nothing," said the traveller,
reassuringly, "only Mademoiselle is a
little feverish. A cold, you know, — I
am sure it is only a cold!"

"Ah, François!" said the Queen, unconscious reproach in her voice, "that
she should have lain so long in the wet
grass yesterday! The pity of it!"

" Tst! tst! why should you distress
yourself?" rejoined the King, "she is
flushed with her nap. See what a
pretty study for ' The Baby Sleep' your
English poet sings of, Monsieur."

Monsieur looked; but he did not think
the coloring of a picture of sleep should
be so feverishly brilliant, nor the blue

shadows under the long
lashes so dark. He
transferred the little
slumberer to Madame's
arms, and saw her car-
ried off to the nursery
with a sigh of relief.

" Mon ami, I wish to
ask your advice on an
affair of business. Can
you spare me half an hour?" asked
François, producing his cigarette-case.
" We can have a chat and a smoke in

the garden, and perhaps you will give us your company to supper ? " and the traveller, assenting, followed his host into the little orchard beyond the Tree of Life.

Here, while the sun dropped slowly from one white cloud peak to another, and the thin shadow crept as slowly round the dial, François told his story, and the young barrister listened, suggested, and advised. He did more, he promised to throw himself, head and heart, into their interests, and win — if steadfast will and tireless energy *could* win — their cause.

" As for your quick French tongue, — well the idioms puzzle me, to be sure ; but I have studied lately, and improved, I will study more, and, if need be, employ an interpreter. Oh, I will get along well enough, and right *is* might, whatever cynics may aver ! "

François laughed, and then looked grave again.

" But, my dear fellow, for you it is a risky undertaking, — there will be much dispute, and supposing we fail —." he paused.   " No, it is hardly fair upon you. You see — " with a flush, — " I am as poor as a church-mouse."

" Bah ! " cried the other, growing crimson too, " of what are you thinking?   Am I a cringing parasite, plotting for my own ends, or am I your friend ? "

" You are a true knight," smiled François, holding out his hand.

" Thank you.   And true knights fought for love, not lucre."

" So?   Then, Sir Knight, when shall we open the campaign ? " asked François, touched by the young fellow's honest kindliness, yet glad to leave an embarrassing subject.

"At once. Let us lose no time and start for Laurienne to-morrow."

"Bien, mon ami, you are red hot! You will burn a hole in their parchment — "

"Let us hope it won't all end in smoke!" laughed the true knight, extinguishing his cigarette; "see, there is Mademoiselle Virginie, beckoning us in."

They walked slowly to the house, and into the kitchen, where supper was prepared. The table, covered with its coarse, white cloth, was set but for a homely meal; yet the traveller thought it looked charming. There was a salad that was a picture of itself in its blue-and-white bowl, with the delicate green of the wet lettuce-leaves, sprinkled with tiny, crisp leaflets of cress, relieved here and there by the creamy yellow of a

hard-boiled egg or the vivid scarlet of
a radish. Around it stood the twisted
loaf, a golden wedge of cheese, and the
cool, glistening pats of butter, fresh
from Virginie's dainty handling.

There were some stuffed tomatoes too,
— ripe, red " pommes-d'amour," — more
substantial than they looked, reposing
in a nest of cress, and a jar of honey.
And in the centre stood a brown jug
filled with roses.

The vine-wreathed lattice was wide
open, and through the transparent veil
of quivering leaves and tendrils the
low sun shone but faintly, so that the
kitchen was half in cool, green shadow,
and half in tremulous, golden light.

Oh, yes, it was all very charming, and
perhaps Virginie, in her faded pink
cotton, with a knot of carnations at the
throat, was the most charming of all.

"SHE WAS STANDING ON TIPTOE BY THE DRESSER."

She was standing on tiptoe by the dresser, to reach down the blue-and-white plates, and though the occupation might be homely, — prosaic even, — it showed off the supple lines of her figure, and the delicate curves of her throat. The traveller almost wished she would stay like that; but when she turned her head, and brought into view the dusky ripples of her hair, and the blood-red carnations against her neck, he thought she looked prettier still. No doubt he was becoming enchanted, along with every one else who lived in the Castle, and the sad, gray hues of his life were giving place to the rose-color of romance.

But one grows hungry, even in romance, and François and his guest did justice to the supper at which Virginie presided, Madame sending many apolo-

gies for her absence. The Princess
was feverish and fretful, — the Queen
must watch and soothe her; but Virginie could take her place, and Monsieur
would understand.

It was late when they rose. Plans
and means had to be discussed, and
when, at length, the traveller left the
Enchanted Castle, twilight had deep-
ened to darkness, and the new moon
hung suspended, like a silver sickle,
above the Tree of Life.

CHAPTER VII.

HOW THE SHADOW FELL UPON THE ENCHANTED CASTLE.

ULLED in the bosom of the night, that baby moon had grown to a beautiful bride, with a golden hoop like a wedding ring around her, and yet the harvest was not gathered in. The Apples of Life were growing over ripe; soon they would be as the Dead Sea fruit of old, yet there they hung, like golden lamps, upon the Tree of Life, and no one came to gather them.

The Dragon, who had guarded them
since first the pale wreaths on the bud-
ding boughs had flushed beneath the
kisses of the spring, all through the
green summer, and into the golden
autumn, — the Dragon lay low in the dust,
at the gate of the Enchanted Castle.
The knight who was to climb among
the branches, and win the treasured
fruit, was fighting, far away, a war of
words.

And the Princess — ah, the Princess! She who had played beneath
the Dragon's protecting pinions, lay in
the shadow, now, of other wings, — the
wings of the Angel of Death.

Through the long day, and in the
silent night, Virginie and Madame
watched by turns beside the little crib.
The quiet nursery echoed no longer
to the childish rhymes and lullabies of

old, nor to the April music of baby laughter and tears. Only the faint moans of fever and the terrible chatter of delirium broke the silence, and now and then a low wail of despair, wrung from the Queen's sad heart.

Virginie stifled her grief in Madame's presence, beating down the rebellious pain, and forcing back all signs of sorrow, till it seemed as though her heart must break with the strain, and the fire of unshed tears would burn into her brain.

The King and the traveller had been gone a fortnight; and so far the old doctor, who came daily from the town, had discouraged the idea of sending for them. The fever must run its course, he said, there was no cause for unnecessary alarm. A man in a sick-room was like a bull in a china-shop; and Mon-

sieur could ill afford to leave his business. No, no, wait a little, and see
what time would do.

But time only fanned into fiercer
flame the cruel fever, till the frail little
life seemed likely to be burned away,
and even the old *médecin* took alarm.

Send for Monsieur now, by all means.
He had certainly meant to act for the
best in advising delay; but now, — ah,
yes, Monsieur must come with all speed,
though even yet he did not despair. A
child's life is like a hot cinder: one
moment it seems extinguished, but a
breath, and, presto, we have it alight
again!

In trembling haste, Virginie wrote
the letter, and ran down the hill into
St. Servans, to post it. She glanced
reproachfully at the Blue Dragon as
she hurried past. Had it not been for

that unlucky sleep in the wet grass, Marie Juliette would still be happy and well. To be sure, there was the will; but what were a thousand châteaux to the life of their love and delight, — the quaint, sweet-tempered little Princess? She had directed her letter to the Château de Laurienne, not knowing where else to send it. They had not heard from François for some time past, and knew not where the trio had gone; for old Petit had insisted on joining his son-in-law, in the firm belief that he was an invaluable witness from the circumstances of his connection with the family, and his having been present at the funeral of the old Count.

For days there came no answer. Madame waited with the dull patience of despair; Virginie with the sickening anxiety of suspense. Morning after morning she stood at the gate, in the chill October dew, watching for the early postman; and there she hurried when evening came, straining her eyes through the dusk till the sea mist floated up the hill, and sent her shivering home, to meet the Queen's questioning glance with the blank look of failure·

Ah, how they felt their poverty now! The journey to Normandy had made lighter still the light purse; and Virginie sighed· as she took it out to pay the weekly bills. There were so many things the Princess needed, that had, till now, been almost unknown in· the Enchanted Castle, — medicine, and wine, and all the necessary luxuries of illness·

As the fever neared its crisis, Monsieur Lécoz became more and more

emphatic in his demands for strengthen-
ing food and wine, and fast as these
increased, the scanty store of coin where-
with to meet them dwindled faster still.
He seemed anxious, too, for the return
of M. de Laurienne ; and Virginie grew
desperate. Madame seemed sinking
into the apathy of hopeless grief. She
never left the nursery, but watched day
and night beside the little sufferer, tor-
tured by the sight and sound of agony
she could not soothe.

On Virginie fell the heaviest burden
of that heavy time. When heart and
brain seemed numb with sorrow, she
must think and act, and scrape and
save, while the poor francs slipped
through her fingers, and little debts
grew daily larger. She alone must
know how hopeless grew the doctor's
face and words ; how hard to glean from

10

them a grain of comfort for the sad
watcher upstairs. And under all lay
the haunting fear of something wrong
in Normandy, — misfortune, illness,
death, perhaps.

" Why do they not write? Why do
they not come?" she cried despairingly,
leaning against the gate,
in the cold gray of the
autumn morning. And
then, with a throb
of hope, she
caught the gleam
of a blue coat
coming up the
lane. Thank God,
the *facteur* at last!

She flew to meet
him, flushed and joyous with expecta-
tion. The man uttered a civil " Bon
jour!" but Virginie did not hear it;

she knew only that he took two white
envelopes from the little wooden box
slung across his shoulder, and put them
into her hand, before he turned and
went, whistling, on his way.

One was from François, written from
the little assize town near Laurienne.
She tore it open, and saw, with a pang
of disappointment, the few hurried
words scrawled in glad haste.

" The suit is won ! "

Ah, God, and was this all ?

No — there was the other letter
fallen at her feet, — a later one, no doubt ;
and she stooped, and picked it up, once
more in a flutter of hope.

Virginie's heart leaped into her mouth
and then fell, cold and heavy as a stone,
while she gazed, with hard, dilated eyes,
at the thin, white packet in her hand.
It was her own letter returned.

For a moment she stood as in a dream, blankly staring at the official stamp on the envelope, and the terrible words, " Not known." Then she ran along the lane down the hill to the little post-office. There were only two francs left in her purse, but this was no time for prudent delay. With trembling fingers she seized a telegraph form, copied the address from her father's letter, and wrote underneath the short, sad summons : —

" Come at once.   Marie Juliette is dying."

It was so early, so very early, surely they could reach St. Servans by night! To-night, the old doctor said, the fever would reach its crisis.   The King would come — *must* come — to see the Princess die!

For in her heart of hearts, Virginie

had no hope of any other ending to this cruel illness. She might force her quivering lips to smile, and her faltering voice to speak cheerfully, when the poor mother turned to her for comfort. But she felt how false were looks and words, and how completely her own heart contradicted them. Yet how could she crush that other tender heart by already casting upon it the shadow of a blow that must too surely fall?

Mimi came trotting across the lawn to meet her, mewing plaintively. Virginie dared not let her enter the sick-room, for it tried Madame too sorely to see the poor pet's distress when her fond pats and purrings failed to win response from the sad little sufferer, who lay unconscious of it all. So Mimi's loving anxiety wrought her banishment, and she was forced to wander, disconsolate, about the garden, or patiently to haunt the nursery door.

"What is that to us — now?" the Queen said bitterly, when Virginie showed her the King's short note.

She sat beside the Princess, her hands lying wearily in her lap, her sad eyes fixed upon a dead rose-branch that creaked and swung outside the window.

"But I hope — I think — he will be here soon," said Virginie, trying to speak brightly, — "perhaps to-night, Mother dear."

"It will be too late," said the Queen, and into her eyes came a look that sent a chill to the girl's heart, and froze the comforting words upon her lips. For drowned in those sad eyes, all hope lay dead, and she knew now that her care

had been in vain. She saw, with a
pang, how pale the Queen had grown,
how loosely lay the wedding ring upon
her finger. With a sob she turned
away and went downstairs to prepare
for the King's coming.

On the dresser lay the book of fairy-
stories, with a leaf turned down to mark
the place.

"Oh, Marie Juliette!" sighed Virginie, smoothing back the crumpled
corner; and she remembered how the
Princess had laughed, that sunny afternoon, when Mimi put her paw across
that very page, and brought the merry
reading to an end.

The doctor came and went and came
again.

"About midnight, Mademoiselle," he
said, the last time, "I will be here again.
It is then that the critical moment

arrives, and the change takes place, for
life, or death.   Pray God it be for life!"

But to Virginie, kneeling in the little
niche beside her bed, where hung the
pure white crucifix, and
the scallop-shell of holy
water, her prayers
seemed vain.   The
suffering eyes of
the sad figure
above her seemed
to look down in
pitiful compassion; no hope was there.
The rosary slipped through her fingers,
and she knelt in silence, looking up
piteously.

Still the sad eyes looked down, so
pure, so pitiful, with such a holy calm,
Virginie's own heart throbbed into rest
as she gazed, and she knelt with folded
hands, in sad submission, before the
carved Christ.

A golden ray that leaped into life on
the walls of the little shrine, and slanting fell upon the foot of the cross,
warned her that it was growing late.
She rose and went, with the sweet peace
still reflected in her face, into the
nursery, to take her turn in watching
beside the Princess.

The Queen looked up, as she gently
took her place, and said, with a caressing
touch, —

"What a comfort you are to me,
Virginie!"

"Thank you, ma mère," said Virginie, simply, kissing the hand that
rested on her shoulder; "and now you
must rest yourself a little, — yes, yes, just
a little! So much depends upon our
care to-night, we must be fit and fresh
for it. See, one hour's sleep, and then a
little coffee will do you so much good!"

She coaxed Madame to lie down upon the couch by the window, covered her with a shawl, and drew the curtains to shut out the level sunset light. Then she went back to her post, and sat, quietly knitting, beside the crib.

The Queen, weary with watching and weeping, fell sound asleep. The sun dropped low, quivered upon the horizon, and went out like a lamp, leaving the room in sudden twilight. There was no sound but the soft click of Virginie's needles, and the mournful creaking of the dead rose-branch against the pane. So still the Princess lay, so soundly slept the tired figure on the couch, so silent sat the other quiet figure in the shadow, they might have been inhabitants of the Sleeping Castle — in the old, old fairy-story — over whose walls the fairy cast her drowsy spell.

Virginie's fingers sped mechanically, and her sad thoughts seemed to move in time with the musical click of her knitting needles, and were almost as monotonous.

" Marie Juliette was dying. Would the King be in time ? "

Between those two ever-recurring ideas her thoughts flew backwards and forwards like a shuttle in the loom. The haunting question came with every few stitches; it was woven over and over again into the woollen stocking : " Would the King be in time ? "

Suddenly into the darkness rose the sound of faint singing, like the tiny, tremulous song of a prisoned bird. As the quavering notes rose and fell, Virginie's heart, listening in the stillness, quivered and vibrated like a harp with broken strings. She dropped her head

into her hands, and her throat shook
with gasping, stifled sobs.

But the little voice quavered on, like
a reed-pipe out of time.

> " À mon beau château,
>   L'on y danse, l'on y danse !
>   Et moi je suis la plus gaie,
>   La plus gaie fillette en France ! "

A great sob broke in upon the last
line, as the crash of a minor bass strikes
discord among the trilling notes of the
treble. The Queen was awake and listening. Virginie caught her breath, and
looked toward the window. Against
the dim background of the white curtain, she could trace the dusky outline
of the Queen, sitting with bowed head
and clinched hands, crying bitterly in
the darkness.

> " Et moi je suis la plus gaie,
>   La plus gaie fillette en France !
>   Tra, la . . . . . . "

sang Marie Juliette, hoarsely, and then stopped suddenly, with a gasp.

Virginie struck a light, and carried it to the bedside. There lay the Princess, struggling for breath, with a wild terror in her beautiful, pathetic eyes, beating the air with helpless, baby hands. Virginie raised her, and held her in her arms till the breath came back, with a long, fluttering sigh, and then laid her gently down again upon the pillow. For a little while the Princess lay panting softly and staring at the light, but presently the weary lids dropped down, and she sank into a heavy sleep.

True to his word, the little doctor came soon after midnight. The Princess still lay in that heavy stupor into which she had fallen some hours before, and he took up his post near the bed,

to watch patiently till the critical moment should arrive.   Beside the pillow
knelt   the   Queen,   praying   earnestly
with trembling lips.   Virginie sat in the
window, leaning her weary head against
the frame, watching for the King.

"Sancta Maria! Ora pro nobis!"
murmured the poor mother, while the
tears fell faster than the beads through
her nervous fingers, "Sancta Maria!
Ora pro nobis!"

Down there in the moonlit garden
stood the Tree of Life, with silver
leaves drooped round its golden fruit,
and from the end of the laurel-walk,
where he lay low in grass and dew, the
fallen Dragon still kept watchful eyes
upon the gate.

The moon, to-night, had thrown off
her veil of mist, and floated in pure
majesty on the unruffled surface of the

"BESIDE THE PILLOW KNELT THE QUEEN."

cloudless sky, — a golden ship, upon a blue night-sea.

But the Princess was floating down a darker tide, into "the land where all things are forgotten."

CHAPTER VIII.

HOW THE KING AND THE TRUE KNIGHT CAME BACK FROM NORMANDY.

SUDDENLY Virginie's listening ear caught the rush of wheels, — or was it the dead rose-branch, brushing the window-pane? She bent her head and listened intently, straining her ears to catch the faintest sound, with her hands clasped over her beating heart lest its throbs might disturb the silence. Ah, *was* it only the dead rose-branch against the pane? No, there it was

again, — crisp, distinct, the distant
crunch of heavy wheels upon the
gravel-drive.

Thank God, they were come at last,
— and not too late! Virginie slid noise-
lessly past the little group by the crib,
unseen or noticed only as a moving
shadow. She stole swiftly downstairs,
feeling her way in the darkness, and
through the stone passage, white and
cold in the light of the moon, where
her own shadow flitted before her on
the wall. Then, with eager, hurrying
steps, into the kitchen, where no light
shone, save the red glimmer of the failing
fire. As she struggled nervously with
the bolts of the door, a fiacre dashed
past the window, and some one leaped
out, and up the steps. Fearful lest the
clang of the knocker should startle the
little sleeper upstairs, Virginie wrenched

open the door, and her father strode
over the threshold.

"Juliette?" he muttered hoarsely.

"Upstairs," murmured Virginie, and
François hurried away.

When she turned again to the doorway, some one else stood on the threshold, tall and dark against the moon;
it was the traveller, and he held out
his hand, saying cheerfully, —

"We are come at last, Mademoiselle."

The tears rushed to Virginie's eyes,
and she caught the kind hand in her
own, with a sob.

"Yes, you are come at last!" she
cried; "but it is late — and our hearts
are breaking!"

The traveller closed the door. He
had sent the fiacre away, and they could
hear the *cocher* calling, "hola!" to his
tired horse, till the cries grew faint in

"AND HER FATHER STRODE OVER THE THRESHOLD."

the distance, and all was quiet again. But Virginie still leaned against the wall, with the tears running down her cheeks. She did not move till her companion spoke, using unconsciously her own words of that night, not very long ago, when he had first come to the Enchanted Castle.

" I am so sorry for you! " he said.

The tender, pitying tone went to Virginie's heart; she covered her face with her hands, and all the pent up agony of weeks burst forth. The tears rained down through her interwoven fingers, and she shook with sobs like a marsh-flower in the wind. The traveller felt very miserable; but he knew it was best to let grief have its way. So he waited, quietly, in the shadow of the hearth, till the passionate weeping ceased, and then went over to Virginie's side.

"Is there nothing I can get you, Mademoiselle? You must be so faint and tired, — a glass of wine, perhaps?"

"No — oh, no," said Virginie, shaking her head; and she smiled a little, sadly through her tears, "in a minute — I shall be quite — all right. Now — let us go to the Princess."

She went on before him, up the stairs and into the nursery.

"Hush!" said the little doctor, looking up, "not yet, Mademoiselle."

The traveller walked over to the window, and stood there looking out. Virginie came and stood at his side, and looked out too, crumpling her wet handkerchief in her hand.

There was the moon, a little higher now. There lay the quiet garden, silvered with her pale kisses, dropped down between the whispering boughs of poplar and of yew.

" Oh, dear God in heaven !" breathed Virginie, softly, " do not let Marie Juliette die !"

She looked toward the little group around the bed. There knelt the King and Queen, side by side, and the old doctor watched near the pillow. Between them lay the Princess, sleeping heavily. As she looked, Monsieur Lécoz quietly raised his hand, and beckoned.

Virginie touched the traveller gently, and together they joined the watchers. What had happened to the Princess? All look of pain, and the hot flush of fever, had left her baby face. It was

white now, so white and still, with the
blue veins thinly traced across the pure,
white brow, like the face of a baby angel
carved in marble.

"Marie Juliette is dead," thought
Virginie, and she looked at the traveller
and then at Monsieur
Lécoz.
They were gazing, with a
smile, at the quiet little
form, and the doctor held
one tiny hand, and nodded
his head to himself. Sud-
denly, with three fitful leaps, the candle
went out. No matter, the moon gave
light enough to see the Princess lying cold and still, in that calm sleep
from which no kiss could wake her.
Virginie sat on, with a dreary wonder
at her heart. Why were they watching
now, when all must be over; and why

was there a smile upon the traveller's face? Was it nothing to him that their Marie Juliette must die?

So the minutes slowly sprang to life, and died, one after another, like tiny bubbles blown into the air. Suddenly a clock from some church spire in St. Servans chimed clearly — two! and as the last stroke shivered into silence, the Princess opened her eyes. The room was all in darkness, save where the little square of moonlight shone, latticed with the shadows of the case-ment. The soft light fell upon the traveller's face, as he knelt opposite the window, and played behind him in a silver halo on the wall. As in the dreamy dawn of consciousness her wak-ing eyes met his, the Princess looked up with a beautiful smile.

"You are a true knight," she said

faintly; "you will rescue a distressed maiden."

The true knight gently took her little wan hand and raised it to his lips. Leaving it still within his big, brown fingers, the Princess turned her head upon the pillow, and fell into a happy sleep.

And next day they gathered in the golden harvest from the Tree of Life.

CHAPTER IX.

"À MON BEAU CHÂTEAU."

ONCE more the Blue Dragon sat in state, keeping guard over the treasures in the drawing-room of the Château de Laurienne.

But surely, not a year ago, he was lying, battered and broken, down in the long grass at the gate of the Enchanted Castle?

"Ah, yes; that was a wonderful story."

When the Princess fluttered back from those cold wings of death, into

her warm nest of life and love, she
found the gates of Fairyland once more
thrown open, and at the portal, grand
and green as ever, sat the Blue Dragon.
For the true knight had rescued the
distressed maiden, and the days of chiv-
alry were not yet dead.

Not with his good sword, nor his pranc-
ing steed had he wrought the change,
but with a paste-brush, and a bottle of
cement, bought at a little shop in St.
Servans. With these talismans he had
set the blue monster's head upon its
neck, had joined the severed claw, and
mended the broken wing. And then
came the master-touch, the piece of
magic that kept the Princess in a state
of happy wonder from morn till night.
You could not see the joins, — not by
the smallest chip, nor tiniest crack,
could you tell that the Blue Dragon
had ever been broken !

For round its massive throat was traced a collar of gold, one broad rippling line, that lay upon the undulating blue like a sunbeam on the water. And the claw was circled with a golden ring that quite dazzled your eyes with its shining. The same fairy touch had spangled the broken wing with stars, and painted a crescent moon upon the tip. Indeed, the Blue Dragon looked more beautiful than ever, and all this gilding meant something, — as much, perhaps, as a Victoria Cross, or the Legion of Honor; for every golden point was an order of merit. He was more decorated than the greatest general who ever lived through a campaign; and one felt quite awed before his starry splendor. Yes, certainly, it had been beautifully done.

The first day that the Princess was

allowed to go out, she was carried, in
her true knight's arms, down to the
gate of the Enchanted Castle.

It was a lovely morning, quite gorgeous with the ripe, rich coloring of latest autumn. What
though the
leaves had
fluttered, like brown
birds, from the bare trees;
they made a shifting carpet of
red and yellow upon the drive, and
lay in drifting heaps about the stone
steps of the porch, and pricked a rosy
pattern out upon the lawn; and the
leafless branches made a beautiful brown
tracery against the sky, so that one
could see, now, what a delicate harp
the wind played upon in the autumn
nights. For when summer songs, with
summer birds, are flown, then comes the

"SHE WAS CARRIED IN HER TRUE KNIGHT'S ARMS."

glorious Æolian music of the wind, —
so sad, so sweet, haunting the bare
trees like the voice of a soul. What
though the garden was no longer gay
with flowers and fruit; there stood
the holly-bushes, like glossy Christmas-
trees hung with rubies, and the brier
sprays, strung with their red berries,
drooped across the way, each a rosary
of scarlet beads. And then so mysti-
cally blue the sky, one could gaze and
gaze into the clear depths as into the
pure eyes of a child; and the crisp air
was like the breath of the sea, — so
cold and fresh and invigorating it
made the heart dance, and the pulses
beat with the mere joy of being.

The Princess made a royal progress
down the garden-walk. Mimi trotted
before, very sleek and demure, with one
eye on the holly-bushes, in case of a

robin; and then Virginie, all aglow with the wind, tripped on, to part the briers and branches, and clear the way of falling boughs. The Princess, in her true knight's arms, came next; and the King and Queen followed after, — the King carrying an extra shawl, lest the wind should prove treacherous, and the Queen blowing kisses whenever the Princess looked back. And so they came to the gate; and there sat the Dragon, glittering in the sun.

They all looked expectantly at the Princess; and the traveller smiled, as he saw the glad rose-color in her cheeks and the shining of her eyes. Mimi walked up to the blue monster, and sniffed about inquisitively for a minute, and then trotted away with a contemptuous whisk of her tail. But that must have been jealousy, for Mimi had no ornaments, — not even a collar and bells!

"Mais que c'est beau!" murmured the Princess, clasping her hands in a quiet rapture, and laughing low, with delight. She would like to stay there for hours, gazing at her dear Dragon; but the Queen demurred. It was cold, and time for Marie Juliette to go in, . she said. So they turned, and now the true knight was his lady's steed, and pranced and galloped back to the house in splendid style; while Virginie ran on before, and Mimi rushed wildly about them, distracted, between the riotous trio and robins and whirling leaves.

But that was nearly a year ago, and now the Blue Dragon had his rights again, which was just as it should be. And François shared them, in the

Dragon's opinion, though I fancy he
was sole master of the Château in his
own. And the pretty Juliette of long
ago was mistress of Laurienne after all.
She made a charming Countess, and
that is only to be expected of a Queen;
for royalty can play many parts, where
" Noblesse oblige " is the motto of
all.

Though the Princess had left the
Enchanted Castle far behind, the charm
of Fairyland was still woven about her,
and she lived in a dainty world of
romance, where, as of old, the Blue
Dragon reigned supreme. Old Petit's
orchards were to her enchanted ground,
for were they not the very gardens of
the fairy-tale, where grew the golden
apples, thick as stars? She would lie
in their tremulous shade all day, looking up, with happy eyes, at the ripening

fruit above, choosing the finest and brightest for the traveller, who still stayed near, for she was very loyal to her true knight. He was all alone in the world now, for his mother had long since gone her way, " to gather her harvest in the Garden of Paradise."

But some one else led the old life in the Château de Laurienne. While the Queen laid aside her homely cares with the big bib-apron, and François exchanged the work of the drawing-master for the pleasant duties of M. le Comte, Virginie clung, with a pretty persistence that was half sweet, half wilful, to the old life and the old ways. She worked as blithely here, where work was play, as in the poor, simple days at St. Servans, — rising with the lark to learn the mysteries of milking and churning, or to practise scales and

"Do, re, mi," before the looking-glass, happy alike in drawing-room or dairy. M. le Comte might wish her to acquire the airs and graces "d' une grande dame," rather than the art of making butter, or the best method of preserving fruit. The pretty grace that comes of birth and true nobility was hers already; but "grande dame" she would never be. Still, she sang for Signor Sofala, and danced for Monsieur Pirouette, and even learned, with half-protesting sigh, to play the guitar, as befits a Demoiselle de Laurienne; but, through all this dainty masquerading, laughed the free, joyous Virginie of old.

Mimi was in high feather at Laurienne. Such milk, such cream, such sport in wood and orchard! What could one wish for more?

So they were all quite content, from

the Princess to her poor puss, Mimi,
and the Dragon, who had kept the key
to all this happiness, sat enthroned in
their midst. Certainly, he had played
his part magnificently; but no one
need be surprised at that, for he
was the gift of a duke.

And the traveller?

This is a romance.
And I think — in romance
— the true knight who
fought for love would win
his own reward. He would
find the beautiful maiden, perhaps, under
the orchard boughs, in the glad harvest-
time, and she would give him the Apple
of Life, in exchange for the golden ring.
And they would be very happy; for he
was chivalrous and brave, and she was
pure and true. As in Mendelssohn's exquisite " Duetto," the tender cadence of

the man's deep tones underflow the ringing treble of the woman's sweeter voice, so, in mingled harmony, their lives would flow — in romance.

And if into the melody there sometimes came the sighing winds of sorrow and the sound of falling tears, the music would not be less beautiful. For life, like a song, perhaps, is sweetest. sung in a minor key.

DEAR DAUGHTER DOROTHY.

BY MISS A. G. PLYMPTON.

With seven illustrations by the author.   Small 4to.   Cloth.

PRICE, $1.00.

DEAR DAUGHTER DOROTHY.

" The child is father of the man," — so Wordsworth sang : and here is a jolly story of a little girl who was her father's mother in a very real way.   There were hard lines for him; and she was fruitful of devices to help him along, even having an auction of the pretty things that had been given her from time to time, and realizing a neat little sum.   Then her father was accused of peculation; and she, sweetly ignorant of the ways of justice, went to the judge and labored with him, to no effect, though he was wondrous kind.   Then in court she gave just the wrong evidence, because it showed how poor her father was, and so established a presumption of his great necessity and desperation.   But the *Deus ex machina* — the wicked partner — arrived at the right moment, and owned up, and the good father was cleared, and little Daughter Dorothy was made glad.   But this meagre summary gives but a poor idea of the ins and outs of this charming story, and no idea of the happy way in which it is told. — *Christian Register.*

ROBERTS BROTHERS, Boston.

A LOST HERO.

By ELIZABETH STUART PHELPS WARD and HER-
BERT D. WARD. With 30 illustrations by Frank
T. Merrill. Small quarto. Cloth. Price, $1.50.

The lost hero was a poor old negro who saved the Columbia express from destruction at the time of the Charleston earthquake, and vanished from human ken after his brave deed was accomplished, swallowed up, probably, in some yawning crevice of the envious earth. The story is written with that simplicity which is the perfection of art, and its subtle pathos is given full and eloquent expression. But noble as the book is, viewed as a literary performance, it owes not a little of its peculiar attractiveness to the illustrations with which it is now adorned after drawings by Frank T. Merrill. — *The Beacon.*

ROBERTS BROTHERS, PUBLISHERS,
BOSTON, MASS.

"The man taught him to beat the drum."

THE JOYOUS STORY OF TOTO.

By Laura E. Richards.

With Illustrations by E. H. Garrett. 16mo. Price, $1.25.

ROBERTS BROTHERS, *Publishers*,

Boston.

SUSAN COOLIDGE'S
POPULAR STORY BOOKS.

Susan Coolidge has always possessed the affection of her young readers, for it seems as if she had the happy instinct of planning stories that each girl would like to act out in reality. — *The Critic.*

Susan Coolidge's books need no commending; they are as tempting as they are sweet and pure. She knows how to make attractive everything she touches; and good literature, good English, does not suffer at her hands, while the refinement of tone and moral fibre are all that could be desired. — *The Literary World.*

Not even Miss Alcott apprehends child nature with finer sympathy, or pictures its nobler traits with more skill. — *Boston Daily Advertiser.*

THE NEW YEAR'S BARGAIN. A Christmas Story for Children. With Illustrations by ADDIE LEDYARD. 16mo. $1.25.

WHAT KATY DID. A Story. With Illustrations by ADDIE LEDYARD. 16mo. $1.25.

WHAT KATY DID AT SCHOOL. Being more about "What Katy Did." With Illustrations. 16mo. $1.25.

MISCHIEF'S THANKSGIVING, and other Stories. With Illustrations by ADDIE LEDYARD. 16mo. $1.25.

NINE LITTLE GOSLINGS. With Illustrations by J. A. MITCHELL. 16mo. $1.25.

EYEBRIGHT. A Story. With Illustrations. 16mo. $1.25.

CROSS PATCH. With Illustrations. 16mo. $1.25.

A ROUND DOZEN. With Illustrations. 16mo. $1.25.

A LITTLE COUNTRY GIRL. With Illustrations. 16mo. $1.25.

WHAT KATY DID NEXT. With Illustrations. 16mo. $1.25.

CLOVER. A Sequel to the Katy Books. With Illustrations by JESSIE McDERMOTT. 16mo. $1.25.

JUST SIXTEEN. With Illustrations. 16mo. $1.25.

IN THE HIGH VALLEY. With Illustrations. 16mo. $1.25.

A GUERNSEY LILY; or, How the Feud was Healed. A Story of the Channel Islands. Profusely Illustrated. One small quarto volume, bound in illuminated cloth. $2.00.

Sold by all booksellers. Mailed, post-paid, on receipt of price, by the publishers,

ROBERTS BROTHERS, BOSTON.

FLIPWING, THE SPY.

A Story for Children.

By LILY F. WESSELHOEFT,

*Author of " Sparrow, the Tramp," " The Winds, the Woods,
and the Wanderer," etc.*

The story represents the action of certain animals, the characters of which are
depicted in accordance with their natures and the exigencies of the story. The object
is to cultivate the love of animal nature. which most children feel, and especially for
such creatures as bats, toads and others, which children are often improperly taught
to regard with disgust. The human characters introduced talk and act naturally, and
the book will be found very entertaining to young people.

16mo. Cloth. Price, $1.25.

ROBERTS BROTHERS, Boston.

By the author of "Dear Daughter Dorothy."

BETTY, A BUTTERFLY.

By A. G. PLYMPTON.

With illustrations by the author.

Square 12mo. Cloth. Price, $1.00.

"AM I NOT FINE?"

Sold by all Booksellers. Mailed by the Publishers on receipt of the price.

ROBERTS BROTHERS, Boston.